Heartland

Tomorrow's Promise

With special thanks to Linda Chapman

To: Linda Tellington-Jones, who first developed T-touch. Her books are inspirational and have helped people to understand horses in a new and enlightened way.

Heartland

❧

Tomorrow's Promise

by **Lauren Brooke**

SCHOLASTIC INC.

New York Toronto London Auckland Sydney
Mexico City New Delhi Hong Kong Buenos Aires

Chapter One

Dark patches of sweat stood out on the bay gelding's coat. He snorted loudly, his eyes darting around the bustling show ground. Lifting up a front hoof, he struck out violently at the grass.

"Gerry!" exclaimed Hannah Boswell, his rider.

Pulling at the reins, the bay pranced in excitement. Hannah turned him in a tight circle, attempting to bring him under control. As the horse whipped his hindquarters around, he almost knocked over a tall, slim girl who was watching.

"Sorry, Amy." Hannah gasped. "He gets really excited when he's about to go into the ring. It feels like he could explode."

"It's OK," Amy Fleming said with a smile. "He just can't wait to show off for the judge. Right, boy?"

Moving in beside the horse's head, she spoke in a low and soothing voice. She put her hand on his warm neck and began to rub his skin in light circles with the tips of her fingers. The gelding blew at her. "Easy, Spartan," Amy whispered. She caught herself quickly, hoping that Hannah hadn't noticed. *No, not Spartan,* she thought. *He's Gerry now.*

But in her mind, Amy knew that to her he would always be Spartan, the beautiful horse that had come to her family's equine sanctuary almost a year ago, after being involved in a terrible road accident. They later learned that he had been stolen. It was Amy and her mother who had tried to rescue him. At Heartland, Amy had helped him recover from the trauma of the accident and had finally reunited him with his real owners — Hannah's family. Of all the horses Amy had helped, Spartan's history was woven closest to her own.

Amy's fingers worked on the bay gelding's neck, and gradually the tension seemed to leave his body. He breathed out deeply and gently nudged her shoulder with his nose.

Hannah watched Amy in wonderment. "How did you do that?"

Amy shrugged. "It's just something my mom taught me." She patted the now calm gelding. "Silly horse," she said affectionately. "If you went into the ring as excited as that, you'd send the fences flying."

"That's true," Hannah said ruefully. "He's knocked a fence down in the jump-off in the last three shows. He gets so psyched up."

"He's probably just nervous. You could try massaging some diluted lavender oil around his nostrils before you tack him up," said Amy. "It's very relaxing. And adding some valerian powder to his feed for a few days before each show should help, too."

"Really?" Hannah said. "That's great. I'll try anything." She looked at Amy. "I can't believe you know all this stuff. Did your" — she hesitated — "did your mom teach it all to you?"

Amy understood Hannah's hesitation. Her mom had been killed in the same road accident that had left Spartan traumatized. After rescuing him from an abandoned barn, they had been taking him back to Heartland through a raging storm when a tree had crashed across the road and upset the trailer. Amy tried to blink the vivid images from her mind. "Yes, she taught me everything," she said quietly.

The loudspeaker suddenly crackled into life. "Next is the jump-off for class 146 — the Marshall and Sterling Children's Jumper Classic. The first qualifying entry is number 203, Dancing Grass Geronimo, owner and rider, Hannah Boswell."

The steward started to open the in-gate. Hannah tightened her reins.

"Good luck, Hannah!" Amy called.

"Thanks!" Hannah replied.

Amy hurried to the stands. Sinking down on a seat, she pushed her long light-brown hair back from her face and watched intently as Gerry cantered into the ring. He looked alert but controlled, his coat gleaming like dark oak in the bright sun. The shortened course of seven jumps looked high but inviting. The class was timed, which meant the horse that jumped the fastest with the fewest faults would win.

As the starting buzzer sounded, a thought flashed through Amy's mind. She realized that she could have been riding him now if he were still at Heartland — if she hadn't worked so hard to reunite Gerry with his original owners. A pang of regret shot through her, but as she watched the horse and rider approach the first fence, the idea was already forgotten.

"Come on, boy," she said, sliding to the edge of her seat. Gerry's stride lengthened, and he soared over the first fence. Amy's upper body moved forward unconsciously, as if she were jumping with him.

Careful now, don't go too fast, or you'll knock one down, she thought as Hannah turned toward the next fence. Gerry sped up in excitement. But Hannah was ready. Sitting back, she steadied him perfectly. Gerry's forelegs snapped tight to his chest. Next, the brush fence, the in-

and-out, the oxer, the wall. He cleared them all with inches to spare.

Amy let out a huge sigh as Gerry galloped through the finish. He was clear and his time was fast. Jumping to her feet, she hurried out of the stand. "Way to go!" she yelled to Hannah. She rushed down the bleachers to meet Hannah at the gate.

"Wasn't he great?" Hannah gasped, patting Gerry's neck as if she were never going to stop.

"The best," Amy agreed.

"I'm so lucky to have him," Hannah said, her blue eyes shining. "He's just so wonderful!"

As if he understood what she was saying, Gerry turned and nuzzled Hannah's leg. Hannah kept patting his neck and smiling.

"I'd better walk him around to cool him off," Hannah eventually said to Amy. She dismounted. "There's not much I can do now but wait and see how the rest of the class goes."

Amy nodded and fell into step beside her.

"Why aren't you competing today?" Hannah asked curiously. "Where's Sundance?"

"He pulled a tendon last week," Amy explained. "Too much roughhousing in the pasture. Our vet, Scott, said I can't ride him for at least three months."

"What a nightmare," Hannah said, shocked.

"I know," Amy replied. She forced a smile. "But Sundance is enjoying it. He's getting totally spoiled."

"Not so good for you, though," Hannah said sympathetically. "You won't get to show this summer at all."

Amy shook her head. "Well, Heartland is so busy right now that I probably wouldn't have had the time, anyway." She spoke positively, but she couldn't help feeling a bit down. Helping damaged horses would always come first with her, but once in a while it was great to ride a horse that didn't need her help. She loved taking Sundance to shows when she got the chance.

Trying to hide her disappointment, she patted Spartan's damp shoulder. "I'm getting a soda," she said to Hannah. "Do you want one?"

"Thanks." Hannah smiled at Amy. "You know, I'm really glad you're here," she said. "My grandparents couldn't come. Chuck — Grandpa's head groom — drove me down, but he's watching dressage. It's nice to have someone rooting for me."

Amy smiled back. *I wish Hannah lived closer,* she thought as she headed across the busy show ground. *We could see more of each other then — maybe even go to shows together.* Amy caught herself. She had to stop thinking like that. She knew she wasn't going to compete in shows again. By next year she will have outgrown Sundance. She just had to accept it.

Finding the food tent, she bought two cans of soda. She was hurrying back to Hannah when a rider on a flashy chestnut trotted right in front of her. Amy stepped back just in time. "Hey!"

As the rider reined in her horse, Amy saw that it was Ashley Grant. Ashley's parents had a high-profile show barn called Green Briar. They had a reputation for training push-button show horses and ponies, using force and strict discipline. Ashley and Amy attended the same high school, but that was all they had in common.

Ashley smirked at Amy. "So, you weren't up for the competition in Large Pony Hunter, Amy?" she said.

"Sundance is lame," Amy said curtly.

Ashley shook her head. "You know it's a shame you don't have a better animal. You used to be pretty good." Smugly, she patted the chestnut's neck. "So, what do you think of Bright Magic? He's a Danish warmblood."

Amy looked at the chestnut. About sixteen hands high with four white socks, he was beautiful.

"He's worth well over five figures," Ashley said. "I'm taking him in Junior Jumpers. Mom thought it was time I moved out of ponies now that I'm almost sixteen. So even when Sundance is sound, we won't be competing against each other." A smile curved across Ashley's beautiful face. "Now you might have a chance for more than second place."

Amy looked at Ashley in disgust. "You just don't get it, do you, Ashley? I don't ride just to win prizes, and I don't care how much your horse is worth."

But Ashley wasn't listening. She was staring at something over Amy's shoulder. "Would you look at that!" she said incredulously.

Amy looked around. A strawberry roan mare was being ridden toward the warm-up ring. Her head was coarse, and her legs stocky as a draft horse's. Her dark-haired rider was slightly built. Amy guessed he was about eighteen. His riding jacket was patched at the elbows, and his tan breeches had obviously seen better days. Even Amy couldn't help but stare. Next to the other entrants, this horse and rider looked totally out of place.

"Hey, you!" Ashley called out to the boy. "You on the roan!" Her clear voice rang out across the ground.

The boy turned, his eyes taking in Ashley on her horse and Amy standing beside her. "Me?" he said, his forehead creasing into a frown.

"Yes, you," Ashley said, rolling her eyes. "What classes are you entered in?"

"Open Jumping and the Six Bar," the boy answered shortly.

Amy felt her eyes widening. Only the best horses competed in those classes.

Ashley raised her eyebrows disbelievingly. "Yeah, right," she said. "What are you really entered in?"

"I told you," the boy repeated, his voice icy. "We're going in the Six Bar in a moment and Open Jumping this afternoon." Glaring at her and Amy, he signaled to his horse to move on.

Ashley laughed. "I don't know who's worse — him or his draft horse!"

The boy swung around, his eyes narrowed. It was clear that he had heard her every word.

"Ashley!" A sharp voice behind them made the girls turn around. Val Grant, Ashley's mom, was marching toward them, her tanned forehead creased with disapproval. "What are you doing, just standing around? I thought I told you to warm up Magic!"

For a moment, Amy almost felt sorry for Ashley, but then she decided Ashley deserved everything she got. As Val Grant approached, Amy left to find Hannah.

Amy and Hannah watched the last few horses in the jump-off, fingers crossed in suspense.

"You did it!" Amy said excitedly as the final horse knocked down the first element of the in-and-out. "You won, Hannah!"

"I can't believe it!" Hannah cried.

The announcer called out the winner's number, and, remounting, Hannah rode into the ring to get the blue ribbon.

After the winning horse and rider had been photographed, Amy walked back with them to their trailer. There was a note from Chuck on the windshield saying that he'd gone to watch the hunters in ring one and that Hannah should call him on his cell phone when she was ready to leave.

Just then a voice coming over the loudspeaker announced that the Six Bar competition was about to start. "I'd really like to see that," Hannah said. "Do you want to watch it with me?"

Amy checked her watch. Ty was picking her up in an hour by the main gate. "Sure," she said. She loved watching Six Bar competitions. The fences — six of them — were set out in a row across the ring, each one a few inches higher than the last. You had to jump all of them, and any horse that jumped clear qualified for the next round, when the fences were raised another couple of inches. The fences kept going up and up until there was a winner. It was a real test of agility and power.

Amy and Hannah loaded Spartan into his trailer and hurried to the main jumping ring, where they found two seats in the stands.

"And now our next competitor, number 365, Brooksby Light, owned by the Travers Company and ridden by Andrew Ramone."

A dapple gray Thoroughbred came into the ring. "He looks kind of like Pegasus, my dad's old show jumper,"

Amy told Hannah. As she watched the horse canter a circle she felt a wave of sadness. Pegasus, her dad's Olympic show-jumping partner, had died last year. Amy still missed him, and a day rarely went by when she didn't pause at the gate to his field and look for a moment at the oak sapling that marked the spot where he was buried.

"Cool horse," someone said in front of Amy.

Amy glanced down and saw that the comment came from a group of junior riders who regularly jumped on the circuit. Not surprisingly, Ashley was sitting in the middle of them.

"Way to go," one of the others commented as the dapple gray cleared all six fences and was ridden out to the sound of applause.

"Our second clear round," the announcer said. "And now number 278, Burning Amber, owned and ridden by Daniel Lawson."

The gate opened, and Amy looked to the top of the ring. Trotting in was the strawberry roan mare that she had seen in the warm-up area. After the last horse, the mare looked plainer than ever.

"It's Daniel," said Hannah as a murmur ran through the crowd.

"You know him?" Amy said.

Hannah nodded. "He lives near our farm. I've seen him at shows. Just watch. Amber's amazing!"

Ashley and her friends were laughing loudly at the strawberry roan.

Amy shook her head as Daniel circled by the stands. She hoped he couldn't hear the rude reaction. Just because Amber didn't look as good as the other horses didn't mean she wasn't able to jump. Amy could see the power and drive in the mare's short back and sloping hindquarters, and there was no doubt about the determination in her eyes. Scowling at Ashley and her friends, Amy found herself inwardly cheering for the roan mare.

"Daniel got her at a sale," Hannah whispered as Daniel signaled Amber to pick up a canter. "No one wanted her. He bought her for next to nothing, and then he found out what a good jumper she was."

The starting buzzer rang. The crowd fell into a hush. It felt as though everyone was tense and waiting for some disaster to befall the rider and his strange-looking horse.

Daniel headed Amber toward the line of fences. Her powerful hindquarters thrust down, and she was over the first effortlessly, then on to the next. She soared over the jumps, her large hooves tucked precisely up underneath her, her body rounding over the bars. Amy thought that something changed when Amber was in the air. The mare's conformation no longer looked awkward. She had an air of elegance over the fence. And all the time, Daniel sat tight to the saddle, his fingers light on the reins, his body perfectly centered over her withers. As he guided her safely over the sixth and final fence, her hooves landed sweetly on the grass, and the crowd burst into applause.

"I told you Amber was good!" Hannah shouted to Amy above the noise. Meanwhile, Daniel gently slowed his horse down and rode out of the ring. There was a look of satisfaction on Amber's face. "Daniel only started competing her two years ago, but he's already upgraded to Open. He could take her all the way to the top."

After watching such a display of jumping, Amy readily agreed with Hannah, and by the time she had watched Amber clear the jumps in the next two rounds, she was sure Daniel and Amber would go far.

By the fourth round, there were only three horses left — Amber, the dapple gray, and a chestnut stallion ridden by international show jumper Nick Halliwell. Amy knew Nick well — last summer she'd cured one of his young horses of its fear of trailers, and under normal circumstances she would have wanted him to win the class. But today she wanted Amber to win. She wasn't alone. The moment Amber came into the ring, the audience exploded. Seeming unfazed by the noise, the roan mare calmly pricked her ears and cantered obediently in a circle. The fences were much higher now, the final fence standing at six feet. The dapple gray had knocked two down. Nick Halliwell had knocked one. If Amber and Daniel could clear all, she would get the blue ribbon.

The starting buzzer went off. Daniel turned Amber into the first fence. In three powerful strides she flew over it. Then over the next and the next, until they soared cleanly over the last jump.

The crowd erupted, jumping to their feet, clapping and cheering. Amber put her head down in a triumphant buck.

"That was amazing!" Hannah said in delight.

Amy stood up, clapping loudly. "Unreal!"

The announcer called Daniel and Amber back in to collect the blue ribbon and a trophy. As the photographers gathered, Amber turned her head and affectionately nipped at her owner's leg. Ignoring the calls to look at the cameras, Daniel bent forward to rub her forehead. Amy smiled at the obvious bond between horse and rider.

Hannah stretched and stood up. "I should get going. Chuck will want to get back."

Amy followed her out of the stands. As they passed the warm-up ring, she saw Nick Halliwell dismounting from his stallion. "Hold on a minute," Amy called to Hannah.

She ducked under the rope. Already three or four people had gathered around Nick, holding programs out for him to sign. He stopped what he was doing and smiled when he saw Amy. "Amy! How're you doing?"

"I'm fine," Amy replied. "I just wanted to say good job."

"Well, we knocked one fence over, but this fella's still young," Nick said, patting the stallion's flanks as his groom led the horse away. "I'd say he did pretty well, considering the competition. Did you see the guy who won?"

"Yeah," Amy said. "Wasn't he great?"

Nick nodded. "He sure was. And what a horse!" He took off his hat. "I'm glad I ran into you," he said to Amy. "I was going to give you a call. One of my youngsters is acting up. He was fine when we first started working him a few months ago, but he's become very resistant recently. He's still green, but I feel like something else is wrong. Scott's checked him over and can't find anything. I thought maybe you could take a look at him."

"Sure," Amy agreed.

"Great. I'll be in touch," Nick replied, turning to sign programs again.

Amy began to hurry back toward Hannah, thinking ahead to what stalls would be free for Nick's horse.

"Watch out!" a voice shouted angrily.

Amy stopped with a gasp. She'd been so consumed by her thoughts that she hadn't seen the roan mare trotting out of the ring and had almost walked straight into her path. Looking up, Amy saw Daniel Lawson glaring furiously at her as he pulled Amber to a stop.

"Why don't you watch where you're going?" he roared from Amber's back.

"I'm — I'm sorry," Amy stammered.

"Do you think you own this place or something?" Daniel demanded. "I can't believe you people."

"What?" Amy was completely taken aback.

"You and your stuck-up friends," he snapped. "You show types are all the same. Looking down at everyone. Laughing at people like me and horses like Amber."

"What? But I . . ."

Scowling angrily, Daniel trotted Amber away. Amy was left staring after him.

Hannah came over. "What was all that about?"

"He just called me stuck-up!" Amy burst out in astonishment. "He accused me of laughing at him and at Amber!"

Hannah stared. "That's weird. I have to admit that he's not very friendly on the show circuit at home, but at least he's not outright rude."

"Well, he sure was just now," Amy said, frowning. "I don't get it."

"Forget it," Hannah said. She glanced around. "I should go and find Chuck. How are you getting back to Heartland?"

"Ty's giving me a lift," Amy answered. She looked at her watch. "Speaking of which, I'd better head over there. I'm supposed to be meeting him at the gate about now. See you, Hannah. Congratulations!"

"Bye!" Hannah called.

Amy raced to the main entrance of the show grounds just in time to see her boyfriend, Ty, pulling up in his pickup into the lot. Seeing his familiar face scanning the crowd for her, Amy felt a quiet happiness well up inside. For years, Ty had been just like an older brother working at Heartland farm with her, but a few months ago they had started dating. It had been difficult at first, dealing with becoming more than friends. But things were going well now, and Amy was certain that their relationship had never been better.

She jogged over to the truck. "Hi!" she said, scrambling onto the seat. "I've had the best day. Hannah and Gerry looked great — they won the Children's Jumper Classic — and I saw Nick Halliwell. He said he might have a horse to send to us. And the Six Bar class was amazing. You wouldn't have believed it. There was this strawberry roan mare. She . . ."

"Amy," Ty interrupted her.

Amy suddenly realized that Ty hadn't reacted to a word she'd said.

"What's up?" she asked, surprised. "Is something wrong?"

"Amy, you've had a phone call . . . from your father."

Chapter Two

"A horse?" Amy said to Ty in disbelief. "What do you mean he's bought us a horse?" Her mind was spinning. Was this for real? "You looked so serious. I thought something awful had happened."

Amy could hardly believe it. Until a visit a few months ago, Amy and her sister, Lou, hadn't seen their father for twelve years. Now Ty was saying that the same man who had once abandoned them had bought them a horse and that it was arriving that afternoon. "Tell me everything," she said excitedly.

"All I know is it's sixteen hands and a warmblood gelding," Ty told her, turning the pickup away from the show ground. "Your dad just called a few hours ago. Lou and your grandpa were out, so I talked to him. He said he's been over here on business. He was looking for young horses to export to Australia, and when he saw this horse he decided to buy it for you and Lou."

"But why?" Amy burst out. "Did he say?"

"No, he didn't say anything else," Ty answered. "He was heading out to see someone and couldn't talk long. He's going to call again tonight."

Amy sank back in the seat. Her dad hadn't said anything to her about coming back to the States, but somehow that didn't seem to matter now. She and Lou were getting a horse. A horse that wouldn't have to be re-homed or go back to its owners like most of the other horses at Heartland. Excitement surged through her, but at the same time she couldn't help wondering why their dad had bought them a horse. After all, it wasn't as if they needed another horse at Heartland. She already had Sundance, and Lou was scared of riding — she had been for twelve years, ever since the riding accident that had ended their father's show-jumping career.

A thought struck Amy as she remembered how, during their father's recent visit, Lou had promised him that she would try to face her fear and start riding again. Maybe he had bought this horse for Lou. Their father was an experienced horseman. It was his business to match horses with riders. He must have realized that they didn't have many horses at Heartland that would be reliable enough for a nervous rider. *Of course,* Amy thought. *That's it. It makes sense.*

"You're awfully quiet," Ty said, looking at her curiously.

"I've just been thinking about why Daddy bought us this horse," Amy answered. "I think it's for Lou. He found a reliable, quiet horse that she can trust, so she can get her confidence back."

"Could be," Ty said thoughtfully.

"I bet I'm right," Amy said, convinced. "I can't wait till it gets here. I wonder what it's like. How old? What color?" A grin spread across her face. What did the details matter? It was a horse of their own — and it was coming to Heartland that afternoon. What could be better than that?

🙞

As Ty drove up Heartland's long drive, the white weatherboarded farmhouse and front stables came into view. Amy saw Lou walking toward the house.

Hearing the pickup, Lou stopped and shaded her eyes. When she saw it was Amy and Ty, she waved.

"Lou!" Amy exclaimed, throwing open the door as soon as Ty had parked. "Ty told me about the horse."

"Can you believe it?" Lou said with a shake of her head. "Apparently, Daddy bought it on impulse." She ran a hand through her short golden hair. "On impulse! How can anyone just buy a horse on an impulse — especially a horse for someone else?"

Amy knew the answer to that, but she guessed that Lou might never understand. Her sister was too practical to act on a whim.

"I mean, it's not as if we need another horse here," Lou continued. "We're busy enough as it is."

Amy followed Lou into the house. Jack Bartlett, their grandfather, was mending a broken halter at the kitchen table, his gray head bent over his work. "I guess you've heard the news," he said, looking up and taking in Amy's excited face.

"Yeah," Amy said. "Isn't it great?"

The creases in Grandpa's weather-beaten face deepened. "I'm not so sure, honey. If we use one of the stalls for this horse, it'll mean we've got one less for the horses that really need Heartland's help." He rubbed his forehead. "I'm sure your father means well, but I wish he'd asked first."

"I can't believe him," Lou said. "He visits once in twelve years, and all of a sudden he's trying to buy us with gifts."

Amy felt stung. "Don't be so mean, Lou. After all, I assume Daddy's bought this horse mainly for you."

A frown crossed Lou's face. "For me?"

"Well, it's not like I need a horse," Amy pointed out. "I've got all the others to ride. I think he's sending a nice school horse for you to learn to ride on again."

Lou looked stunned. "Gosh," she said. "Do you really think so?"

"That's what I figure," Amy replied. She saw a look of wonder enter Lou's blue eyes.

"Well, I *have* been meaning to start riding again," Lou said thoughtfully, "but I've put it off because I didn't want to upset any of the rescue horses. I'm just too nervous to get back on. It would be different if we had an easygoing horse that was sensible."

"It'll be perfect, Lou," Amy enthused. "I'll help you at first. We can go for rides together."

"Now don't start making too many plans," Jack added hastily. "We don't know anything definite about this horse yet."

"No," Amy said, grinning at Lou. "But I can't wait to find out!"

✍

Leaving Grandpa and Lou in the kitchen, Amy went up the yard to deal with her chores. She thought about the imminent arrival. In her mind's eye she saw a bright bay with a noble head and kind eye — perfect for Lou to ride. It would probably be about twelve years old, still in its prime, but past the stage of being headstrong.

Amy remembered the look of surprise and happiness on Lou's face when she had told her that the horse must be for her. Although her sister had never said anything directly, Amy was sure that Lou thought their father had chosen Amy as his favorite. Amy could see why Lou would think that after Amy had bonded with him over their memories of Pegasus. Nonetheless, she knew it wasn't true. But it still explained why Lou had looked so pleased at the thought of their father sending this horse for her. It would seem to be solid evidence that he really did care.

Amy reached the brick-walled stables and went over to Jake, the Clydesdale.

"How are you doing, big guy?" she said, stretching her hand into his stall.

"I'm OK, thanks," a voice answered, and Amy jumped. The tall figure of Ben Stillman, Heartland's other stable hand, appeared around the side of Jake.

"Got you." He grinned, seeing her surprised face.

Amy laughed and opened the stall door for him. "Very funny!"

"You can't tell me that you don't expect one of the horses to answer back someday," Ben said, leaving the stall. "You talk to them just like they're human."

"So?" Amy scratched the blaze on Jake's forehead. "They listen better than most people."

Ben shook his head at her. Before he had started working at Heartland seven months ago, he'd worked at his aunt's large Arabian farm where the horses, although treated well, were essentially considered part of a business. He was gradually adapting to Heartland's ways, but Amy doubted whether he'd ever be as crazy about horses as she and Ty were. Well, except for his own horse, Red. Ben was completely devoted to him.

"So, how was the show?" Ben asked, locking the bolt on Jake's door.

"Great," Amy said, helping him collect the empty hay nets from the other five stalls in the row. She told him about the Six Bar and how Amber and Daniel had won the crowd's affection, along with the trophy. "But Daniel's got a real attitude problem," she continued, telling Ben how he had lashed out at her after the class.

"You get all kinds of weird people at shows," Ben said. "And some of them don't deal with the competition well. Don't let it get to you."

Amy nodded. Ben knew what he was talking about. He regularly entered Red in Jumper classes. "Did you miss not going to the show?" she asked curiously.

Ben had planned to go in the High Prelim division but decided to scratch his entry after Red had some rough practice days a few weeks earlier.

"It was the right thing to do," Ben said as they walked up the yard together. "Red's confidence is coming back now. He's been solid for the last few days, but it would have been wrong to throw him straight into a rated show like Meadowville. I'm going to start him off at a smaller place — there's one next week that I've entered."

They reached the feed room. "Do you want a hand with the hay nets?" Amy asked.

"It's OK," Ben answered. "You should go see Sundance. He's been standing at his stall door half the morning, looking very neglected."

"Neglected!" Amy exclaimed indignantly. "I spent more than an hour with him before I went to the show, hosing his leg with cold water and massaging lavender oil into his neck!"

Ben grinned. "I get the feeling that pony is enjoying being pampered. He'll milk that pulled tendon for all it's worth."

Amy went to the twelve-stall barn. Just as Ben had said, Sundance was looking over his stall door. Seeing her, he lifted his buckskin head and whinnied loudly.

"Hi there, boy," Amy whispered as she reached him. Sundance lipped at her hands and, finding them empty, began to nuzzle at her pockets. Amy fed him the crumbly remains of some alfalfa cubes and unbolted his door to go inside the stall. "So, how's that leg?"

Crouching down, she unwrapped the bandage. Underneath there was a blue pouch of gel. When Amy had put it on Sundance that morning, it had come straight from the freezer and was ice-cold, but now it was warm to the touch. Still, the tendon seemed less swollen than it had this morning.

"Time to change your dressing," Amy told Sundance. The pony had lowered his head and was inspecting his foreleg with his muzzle. Amy gathered up the bandage, foam pad, and gel pack. "I'll be back in a minute."

As she left the stall, Sundance pushed his head against the door. "Sorry," Amy sighed, knowing what he meant. "But you can't go out into the field. You've got to rest that leg."

Sundance wasn't used to being confined to his stall all day. The horses at Heartland were usually turned out in small groups for at least five hours. It made them happier if they were allowed to indulge their natural instincts to graze and socialize.

Sundance nudged at the door again, but Amy pushed back the bolt. If he went outside, he might further injure himself. "You're my patient," Amy said affectionately, "and it's stall rest for you."

She got the things she needed and rebandaged his leg, wondering whether there was anything else she could do to help him recover. She was already feeding him comfrey, buckwheat, and meadowsweet, all good for healing tendon injuries. She thought about the aromatherapy oils in the tack room cupboard. Maybe black pepper oil would help as well.

She went to a stall a few doors down, where Ty was grooming Dancer. He was working quietly, a preoccupied expression on his face.

"Do you think there's anything else I can do to help Sundance?" Amy asked as she leaned over the door.

Ty seemed to shake himself out of a dream. "What?" he answered, as if he hadn't heard her properly.

Amy frowned. It wasn't the first time that she had caught Ty looking preoccupied in the last few weeks. She wondered if he had something on his mind.

"Are you OK?" she asked.

"Yeah," Ty replied. He quickly changed the subject. "I guess you could try black pepper oil. There are probably some other oils that would work. Do you want to take a look at the notebooks?"

Amy nodded and they went to the tack room. There, they began to leaf through her mom's notebooks on natural remedies, looking for information on tendon injuries.

"Here's something," Amy said. "Once the initial swelling has died down, heat massage with eucalyptus, black pepper, and lime oils can help to stimulate the blood flow to speed the natural healing process."

"I found one that says almost the same thing," Ty said. "But it also suggests using peppermint oil."

"I can't believe how much there is on tendon injuries," Amy said, sifting through some loose papers.

Ty sighed. "Sometimes I wonder if I'll ever know half as much as your mom did."

Amy felt her chest tighten. She didn't want to talk about her mother — especially right now, when it was bringing back so many painful thoughts. "These notes say that magnets can help speed up the healing," she said quickly. "I've heard about that. Maybe we should give it a try."

Ty let Amy change the subject without saying anything. "Why not ask Scott when he comes tomorrow?"

"Sounds good," Amy replied.

Ty smiled. "We'll get Sundance better," he said, taking her hand. "You'll see."

A feeling of reassurance spread through Amy. That was the best thing about Ty, she thought happily as she gathered up all the notebooks. He understood her — and Heartland. He wasn't just someone she was dating, he was her best friend, too.

Amy and Ty were sweeping the feed room floor when Ben appeared in the doorway. "Guess what just pulled into the driveway."

Throwing down her broom, Amy went to the doorway. A large white trailer was making its way toward the farm. "It's the horse! I'm going to get Lou and Grandpa!" she said, racing back to the house.

Lou was setting the table for supper.

"The horse is here!" Amy shouted. "Quick! Come on."

Grandpa and Lou followed Amy outside just as the truck pulled up in front of the house.

As Amy went over, the cab door opened and the driver

jumped out. He was holding a clipboard. "Hi. I've got a horse to deliver to" — he consulted his notes — "Amy and Lou Fleming."

"That's me!" Amy exclaimed. "I mean us. I'm Amy Fleming." She was so excited that she could hardly get her words out straight. What was the horse going to be like? What color? A bay like she'd imagined earlier? Or maybe a chestnut?

The driver held out his hand. "Pleased to meet you. I'm Marvin Campbell." He nodded to a woman who was getting out of the cab. "And this is my codriver, Heather. She keeps me awake."

Heather smiled. "Let's get him unloaded."

Amy nodded and was joined at the side of the trailer by Grandpa, Lou, Ty, and Ben. They all stood watching as the heavy ramp swung down.

A gasp left Amy. A young dapple gray horse was standing at the top of the ramp, an amazing horse that was the exact image of her father's old show jumper, Pegasus!

Chapter Three

Amy stood rooted to the spot. Every nerve ending in her body felt like it was on fire.

With a snort, the beautiful gray horse tossed his head, the muscles in his neck rippling under his satin skin.

"Easy now," Marvin said, oblivious to Amy's shock. "Down we go." Clicking his tongue, he led the gelding down the ramp. As the horse's hooves clattered onto the gravel drive, he swung around, his head high, his ears pricked.

Marvin and Heather started to remove the horse's traveling wraps, and Amy began to notice the differences between this horse and Pegasus. He was smaller than her father's old show jumper — just sixteen hands. His head was more dished, his nostrils more delicate, his ears more finely fluted. But in every other respect they looked very similar — gray dapples on a snow-white coat, a dark gray mane, and a silvery waterfall of a tail. Most of all, Amy felt they shared something that couldn't be pinpointed — something that shone through the horse's bright eyes.

And in that moment, Amy knew that the horse standing in front of her — so young, so spirited — wasn't a quiet school mare to help Lou ease back into riding. Amy turned around. Lou looked stunned. Grandpa and Ty appeared equally amazed. Only Ben, who was less aware of the family tensions, seemed at ease. He looked at the gelding with genuine admiration.

"That's some horse!" he said.

Amy could only nod. As she did so, the horse stretched his neck toward her, his nostrils wide. Amy held out her hand, palm up, and he sniffed at it, his soft dark eyes looking at her curiously. Then he lifted his muzzle to her head. He snorted and then pulled at her hair with gentle lips.

"Hey!" Amy protested, finding her voice at last. She caressed his neck. "Hello, beauty. Welcome to Heartland."

The horse breathed out into her face and then nuzzled hopefully at her hands, just like Sundance did. Amy smiled and stroked his soft nose.

"I'll get the papers for you," Marvin said, handing the lead rope to her. "He's called Summer Storm — goes by the stable name Storm, I believe. There's tack and blankets with him as well. This horse comes fully equipped," he said, glancing around at Heather, who was coming down the ramp with an armful of blankets and pads. "Where do you want all this stuff?"

"I'll show you," Ben said. "That OK, Amy?"

Amy nodded. She was hardly able to drag her eyes away from Storm when Marvin put the lead in her hand so he could go up to the cab to get the papers.

For a moment, none of them seemed to know what to say.

It was Grandpa who spoke first. "Well, he's not exactly what we were expecting, is he?"

Ty's face looked troubled. "He's a show horse. There's no doubt about that."

"He's beautiful, though," Amy said, her eyes shining as Storm pushed his head against her.

"Yes, but he doesn't belong at Heartland," Ty said, patting Storm gently. "What are we going to do with a horse like —" He broke off when Marvin came back.

"The papers," he said, holding them out. "There's a letter in there as well, from Mr. Fleming."

Lou stepped forward. "Thanks," she said, taking them. Her face was composed, but Amy heard a tremor in her voice.

"Lou," Amy began, looking at her as Marvin started to carry the remainder of the tack to the barn "I . . ." She broke off. She didn't know what to say. If only she hadn't suggested that this horse might be for Lou. "I'm really . . ."

"Let's see what the letter says," Lou interrupted in a diplomatic tone. She took the papers out of the plastic folder. Amy could see that there were registration details and an envelope from her father. Storm pulled at the lead rope and started to dig impatiently at the gravel with one front hoof.

"Hush," Amy said quickly.

"Here," Ty said. "You look at the papers with Lou. I'll walk him around. He's bound to be stiff from the drive."

Reluctantly, Amy handed Ty the lead rope. She didn't want to let go of Storm, but her curiosity was intense.

"He's seven years old, a Trakehner cross English Thoroughbred," Lou said, reading aloud as Ty walked Storm around the driveway.

Amy nodded. That made sense. The Thoroughbred in him was what made him look so much like Pegasus. The Trakehner — a Prussian breed — explained his slightly dished face, elegant arched neck, and fluid movement.

"He was imported from Germany when he was two by a trainer in Florida," Lou said. "He's had three homes since then." She opened the envelope and read the letter out loud.

> *"DEAR LOU AND AMY,*
> *I hope you like Storm. As soon as I saw him,*

I knew I had to buy him — he looks so much like Pegasus, and he can certainly jump. I was going to take him back to Australia with me but then I thought of you and he seemed so perfect. I couldn't help but notice that Amy's outgrowing Sundance and needs a new horse — one with talent that matches her own — and Lou . . ."

Lou faltered for a moment. When she continued, her voice barely above a whisper, she read,

"I'd like to think that one day you'll be able to compete on him, too. I'm sure that as soon as you start to ride again, you'll become just as fearless and competitive as you used to be. You're such a natural.

I'll call you tonight and answer any questions you have. Storm's a good horse. He's won more than $5,000 in prize money in Jumper classes. But I know that sort of thing doesn't matter to you — you'll love him no matter what, my two wonderful girls. I hope you like your present!
Love always, Daddy."

There was a silence. Amy looked at Lou. Oh, how could Daddy have gotten it so wrong? He'd obviously meant well, but he'd completely misread the situation. He was the one who was fearless when it came to horses, and he simply couldn't understand that Lou was genuinely scared of riding now.

Jack was looking from Amy to Lou. "So what are we going to do?" he asked.

"Do?" Amy asked, uncertain of what he was suggesting.

"Well, we can't keep him," Grandpa said, glancing at Lou.

Amy stared. "What?"

"Your father meant well, Amy," Grandpa said gently, "that's obvious. But Ty's right. Heartland isn't the place for a horse like Storm."

Amy's voice rose. "But we can't send him back!"

"We don't have the money to support a competition horse," Grandpa spoke calmly.

"Well, if we can't afford it, I won't enter him in any shows," Amy said stubbornly.

"But, honey," Grandpa said, shaking his head, "that wouldn't be fair to the horse. All you have to do is look at Storm to see that he's been bred to compete, and if he has the talent your father suggests, then it shouldn't be wasted. You know how expensive it is to enter competitions — there's the riding association dues, the class fees, the travel, not to mention the cost of boarding. We can't afford that sort of thing. And what about the time? You're busy enough as it is."

"I'll find time," Amy said, looking desperately at Storm. "And I won't go to big, expensive shows. Grandpa, please, we can't send him back. He's Pegasus, can't you see that?"

Her grandfather's forehead furrowed. "I know he looks like Pegasus, but keeping him won't bring Pegasus back." Grandpa looked at Lou. "What do you think we should do, Lou?"

Amy's heart sank. She had a feeling she knew exactly what her sister was going to say.

But to her surprise, she saw that Lou was looking uncertain. "Let's not be too hasty, Grandpa," she said. "I mean, I'm never going to show Storm, no matter what Daddy thinks. But it's not fair to expect Amy to give him back. She's outgrowing Sundance, and although none of us has the time or money to compete a horse on the A circuit, maybe we can manage it on a smaller scale. There are lots of shows within traveling distance." She glanced at Amy. "I know I don't always see these things the way you do, that I treat horses more as a business, but this is different. I don't think you should have to send Storm back unless you want to."

"Oh, Lou!" Amy had never loved her sister more. "Thank you!"

Lou looked at Grandpa. "Is that OK, Grandpa?"

Grandpa cleared his throat and reached his hands into his pockets. "I guess so. He's a gift from your father, and I know how much that means to you both. You don't have to send him back if you don't want to. But" — he looked at Amy with his blue eyes — "I want you to promise that if having Storm here doesn't work out, then you'll put his happiness before your own."

"I promise!" Amy said, her eyes shining. "But he will be happy here. I know he will! I'll find time to take him to some shows, and Lou, you'll ride him, too, won't you?" She saw the uncertainty on Lou's face. "I mean, not immediately, but as you get more confident. He'll be your horse as much as mine."

"Maybe," Lou said quietly.

Amy kissed Grandpa and her sister, then ran over to see Storm. He shied at her sudden approach, and she stopped immediately. "It's all right, boy," she said, holding out her hand. He sniffed it and relaxed. "We're keeping him!" Amy told Ty in delight. "And I'm going to be able to take him to local shows. Daddy said in the letter that he's won lots of money in stakes classes." Excitement shone in her eyes. "Oh, Ty, isn't this great?"

Before Ty could answer, Ben, Marvin, and Heather came down the yard.

"It's all taken care of," Marvin said cheerfully. "Everything's unpacked."

Heather looked around admiringly. "This is a great place. Ben was just showing us around."

"Would you like some coffee before you go?" Grandpa offered.

"We have to get going — it's a long trip back," Marvin said. "But thanks for the offer." He patted Storm. "Hope the young fella settles in all right. He's quite a horse."

They got back into the horse trailer, and soon it was turning out of the driveway. Lou and Grandpa went back into the house, and Amy led Storm up the yard to the empty stall next to Jake. The hay net was already full and the straw bed deep.

"This is going to be your new home," she told him as she unfastened his halter and let him nose around the stall. "You'll like it here. I know you will." Storm came over to her and stood happily while she scratched his neck. Amy looked at him in wonder. This was a new experience for her. The horses that came to Heartland were almost always damaged or disturbed, and it often took a long time to build up their trust. But here was Storm, fresh out of the trailer and already so affectionate. He had obviously been treated well all his life. She kissed him and went to find Ty.

He was in the feed room with Ben. They were talking about something but broke off as Amy came in.

"So, what do you think of Storm?" Amy said.

Ben glanced at Ty, and Amy suddenly knew that had been their topic of conversation.

"I think he's great," Ben said. "Your dad sure knows how to pick them. You are going to show Storm, aren't you? I mean, you have to."

"Yeah, I guess — did Ty tell you he's won more than five thousand dollars in jumper classes?"

"Well, you can come to shows with me anytime. It'd be great to have the company," Ben told her. He glanced at his watch. "I'd better go. My mom's coming over tonight. I'm supposed to be making dinner, and I still have to go to the store. See you guys tomorrow."

"See you," Amy and Ty replied at the same time.

As Ben left the feed room, Amy turned to Ty. "Well?"

Ty still didn't say anything.

Amy saw his hesitation and frowned. "What?"

"Nothing," Ty replied. "It's just," — he shook his head slightly — "we're so busy, Amy. When will you have the time to compete Storm?"

"I'll make time," Amy said. She could see the worry in Ty's eyes. "I'll still do just as much here with the horses," she told him. "I'll just have to get up earlier or do more in the evenings, but I will do everything."

"But how?" Ty said. "You work all out as it is. You already give it everything you've got."

"It'll be OK," Amy insisted. "I'll find the time. Storm

is worth it." She took his hand, her eyes beseeching him. "Ty, please — be happy for me."

To her relief she saw him smile — a slightly worried smile, but a smile nevertheless. "OK," he said.

Feeling relieved, Amy sighed. "I wish I hadn't said anything to Lou about Storm being for her. I think she was kind of excited about the idea of having a horse to ride."

"She can still ride one of the others," Ty told her. "How about Dancer? She's healthy now, and she's so gentle and has smooth gaits."

Amy considered his suggestion. Dancer, a paint mare, arrived at Heartland after she'd been found half-starved in a tiny field, with her front legs hobbled together. At first, she had been nervous around people, but as they nursed her back to health they had restored her trust. They'd only been riding her for a few months, but Ty was right.

"Yeah," Amy said, nodding. "I hadn't thought of Dancer."

"Lou could start on her and then move on to some of the others — even Storm, when she feels ready for a challenge," Ty said.

Amy felt much happier. "That sounds good, and I can help. It was so wonderful of her to let Storm stay. I want to do something for her. I'll get her to ride Dancer — that's a great idea."

🙋

That evening after supper, their father, Tim Fleming called. "Daddy!" Amy exclaimed, as she heard her father's English accent on the other end of the phone. "Thank you so much. Storm's amazing!"

Her father laughed with pleasure. "You like him?"

"He's perfect!" Amy replied.

"The second I saw him I knew he'd be a great match for you. Think of him as my way of making up for all those birthday and Christmas presents you never had. Is Lou pleased?"

Amy hesitated. "Yeah, sure." Quickly, she changed the subject. "I can't wait to get on him, Daddy. He looks like he'll be amazing to ride."

Just then Lou came down from her bedroom. She had her makeup bag in her hand. "Lou," Amy said, beckoning to her. "It's Daddy."

She handed the phone over and hung around in the background as Lou spoke to their father. As she had expected, Lou was reserved in her thanks. "It's really very generous of you. He must have cost a fortune." There was a pause. "Yes, well, I'm sure Amy will get a lot of pleasure from him." Another pause. "Yes, and me, too," Lou said, but Amy could hear that her voice lacked conviction. "I'd better go," Lou said quickly. "I'm going out with Scott tonight. See you, Daddy — and thanks again."

Amy took the phone from her. "So," she said eagerly, sitting down in a chair and getting ready for a long conversation. "Tell me all about Storm. Where did you see him? What classes has he been jumping in? Who's been riding him?"

❧

Half an hour later, Amy hung up the phone. Ty had popped his head into the kitchen to say good night, and Lou had left to see Scott. Amy stretched. Her head was buzzing with information about Storm. He had been bred in Germany, then imported by a well-known hunter-jumper barn that had shown him in hunter classes until he had been sold to a client. Storm had then competed in the Amateur-Owner Jumper division and had won often. Tim had said that as soon as he saw Storm jump he knew that he was something special. That, and the way he looked so uncannily like Pegasus were the two factors that made Tim decide to buy him for Amy and Lou.

Amy took a fresh gel pack from the freezer and went outside to rebandage Sundance's leg for the final time that evening. As she walked toward the barn, Storm came to his stall door and looked out. In the evening light, he looked more like Pegasus than ever, and Amy felt a shiver run through her.

She walked over. "Hey, boy," she said softly. "What do you think of your new home?" He nuzzled at her hands and she stroked his nose. "You're going to be happy here. I promise." She kissed him and went to Sundance's stall.

Although it was still light outside, the barn was dim. Amy turned the lights on. Several of the horses snorted in surprise but then continued to munch on their hay nets. Sundance nickered softly as she approached.

"Hi, there," Amy said, caressing his ears and rubbing his forehead.

She let herself into his stall and reapplied his bandage with the fresh ice pack. As she did so, she told him about Storm.

"You'll like him," she said, and then she made a face. Who was she kidding? Sundance didn't like other horses — and there weren't many humans he would tolerate, either. As Amy stroked him, she couldn't help thinking how much harder his life had been than Storm's.

She thought about the other horses in the stalls. All of them had suffered in some way and had come to Heartland to be healed. *Ty's right,* she suddenly realized. *What kind of place does a horse like Storm have here?*

But as quickly as the thought arose, she squashed it. He was a gift from her father, and she wouldn't give him up. Leaning against Sundance, she let her hands work in T-touch circles on his golden neck, her fingers pushing his skin in small circles, just as she had done with Gerry that morning. She worked her way up his neck and toward his head, her fingers moving over his muzzle, gums, and up to his ears. Sundance sighed happily and lowered his head. Amy felt herself relaxing and her mind cleared.

❧

When Amy finally made her way back to the house, she felt calm and refreshed.

"Horses settled?" Grandpa asked as she kicked off her boots.

Amy nodded.

"I thought we'd just have a cold supper," Grandpa said, nodding to the kitchen counter where he had put out a baked ham, potato salad, and coleslaw.

"Great," Amy said, with a sudden yawn. "Do you want me to do anything?"

"Just sit down." Grandpa started to bring the food over to the table. "It's been some day, hasn't it?"

Amy nodded. It seemed a very long time since she had watched Gerry win the jump-off that morning.

Grandpa sat down. "Amy," he said slowly, "I know there's a lot going on just now, but there's something I've got to talk to you about. I'm sure you're aware that it's the anniversary of your mom's death in a little more than three weeks."

Looking at her plate, Amy suddenly felt sick. She put

down her knife and fork. "Like I could forget," she said in a low voice.

"I thought maybe we could visit the cemetery to lay some flowers at her grave — just you, me, and Lou — and maybe Scott and Ty. It could be real simple and quiet."

Amy bit her lip and nodded. She'd been trying so hard not to think about the approaching anniversary, but every day she awoke with a heavy feeling that it was one day closer, and every day she kept thinking if only . . .

If only she hadn't persuaded her mom to go and rescue Spartan that night. If only there hadn't been such a storm. If only the tree hadn't fallen.

Grandpa looked at her and seemed to sense her disquiet.

"Let's eat," he said quietly, squeezing her hand. "We can talk about it another time."

Chapter Four

❧

"You are so lucky," Soraya said to Amy as they stood by the water fountain the next morning at school. Amy had been telling her all about Storm. Soraya held back her shoulder-length black hair at the nape of her neck and bent for a drink. "Now why can't I have a long-lost dad who buys me a show jumper?"

"Because you've got a happy, sane family," Amy grinned. She knew that Soraya, with her settled family life, didn't really envy her.

"True, there's that," Soraya said, releasing her hair so that it bounced onto her shoulders. "But I wouldn't mind if my folks decided to buy me a horse — any horse."

Amy looked at her sympathetically. Soraya's greatest

47

disappointment was her father's constant refusal to let her have a horse.

"You know you can ride at Heartland anytime," Amy told her.

"Yeah," Soraya said. "I do." Her brown eyes twinkled suddenly. "Of course, you realize that's the only reason I'm friends with you."

"I solved that one long ago," Amy said with a laugh.

They smiled at each other, knowing that after being best friends for seven years there was little about the other that they hadn't figured out.

Just then the bell rang. "Come on," Soraya said. "We've got to get to class."

When Amy got home from school that day, the sight of Storm looking over his stall door gave her heart a jolt. She went over to see him, stroking his neck. "We'll go for a ride in a little while," she told him, excitement swirling through her.

Storm lifted his muzzle to her face and blew down his nostrils at her, his dark eyes trusting and affectionate.

Amy kissed him on the nose and then ran to the house to get changed. Once she was dressed in her old jeans and T-shirt, she went to find Ty to catch up on the day's news. He was in the training ring, riding Major, a boarder whose owner had sent him to Heartland in hopes that he could be cured of his bucking habit.

Seeing Amy, Ty reined the bay gelding in and rode over to the gate.

Amy climbed onto the fence and called out, "He looks like he's going well."

Ty nodded. "He hasn't bucked at all today." He patted the bay's neck and filled Amy in on what had been happening. "We've still got to work Hector, Mercury, Maddison, Jasmine, and Spring — and Sundance could use a fresh ice pack sometime soon."

"I'll go do that now," Amy said. "Then if you do Hector and Ben does Mercury, I'll ride Maddison and Spring, and Soraya can ride Jasmine when she gets here."

"What about Storm?" Ty said. "I thought you were going to ride him."

"It can wait," Amy said, trying not to sound disappointed. She was desperate to get on Storm, but she really shouldn't ride him when there was work still to be done, especially when she'd promised Ty only the day before that she wouldn't let Storm interfere with her other work.

"It's OK," Ty said, seeming to read her mind. "Ride Storm first."

"You don't mind?" Amy questioned.

Ty shook his head. "I kind of want to see him go."

"I know. I can't wait! Thanks, Ty!" Amy said in delight, heading to the barn.

Before tacking up Storm, Amy went to Sundance's stall. She was relieved to find that the swelling had reduced considerably. Amy ran her fingers gently over the damaged tendon. Although it was warm, it was nowhere near as hot as it had been when he had first pulled it.

"I'm sure it's getting better," she told Sundance as she rewrapped his leg with a fresh ice pack. "We'll have to see what Scott says when he comes tomorrow."

Giving Sundance a last pat, she got a grooming kit and headed for Storm's stall. She had just finished brushing him when Soraya arrived. "Oh, Amy, he's gorgeous!" she exclaimed as she came into the stall.

Amy felt a glow of pride. "I know."

"And he's so much like Pegasus," Soraya said as the affectionate gray gelding nuzzled at her hands.

"I just hope he jumps like him, too!" Amy said.

After tacking up Storm, Amy led him out to the training ring. Hearing his hooves on the path, Ben and Ty joined Soraya at the gate.

"We'll just take it easy today," Amy said as she mounted.

Gathering up her reins, she squeezed with her calves. Storm moved forward instantly, his mouth reaching for the bit, his hindquarters pushing forward. With the lightest touch, he changed direction, circled, backed up, and halted. Amy felt a sense of exhilaration flooding through her. She had never ridden such a well-schooled horse. She asked him to trot and then canter.

Storm moved effortlessly, his paces smooth and flowing. He was so powerful, so athletic. They did flying lead changes. He countercantered without any hesitation. Amy felt that with the smallest shift in position, she could make him do anything she wanted. There was a single vertical in the middle of the ring, almost four feet high. Amy didn't think twice. Forgetting that she'd been going to take things slowly, that normally she'd warm up a horse over smaller fences first, she turned Storm toward it. His stride lengthened and he took off. For one wonderful moment, Amy felt as if she were flying, and then they landed sweetly on the other side.

"Good boy!" Amy exclaimed, patting him. She cantered him over to where Ty, Soraya, and Ben were standing.

"Wow!" Soraya said, her eyes wide.

"He's some horse, Amy! Everything your dad said," Ben exclaimed. "Do you realize how far you could go on him? USET, World Championships, even the Olympic Games!"

A grin stretched across Amy's face. "Like any of that's going to happen," she said. But inside her, a dizzy delight was pounding through her blood. Storm was more than just a good jumper — he was something truly special. As she patted his neck, a dream she'd had when she was younger came back to her — the dream that one day she'd be a famous show jumper just like her mom and dad. She knew that Ben had only been teasing, but maybe, just maybe, she and Storm could make it to the top!

Get real, Amy told herself, trying to be sensible.

"Are you going to jump him again?" Ben asked.

Amy shook her head. "I'll make that do for his first day. I might take him out on the trails for a bit, though. We can go out together, Soraya, if you want to ride Jasmine."

"Definitely," Soraya said. "I'll go tack her up."

"I'll give you a hand," Ben offered.

"Thanks." Soraya smiled at him. As they walked off together, Amy suddenly realized that Ty hadn't said anything since she came over to the gate.

"What do you think, Ty?" she asked. She saw he was looking troubled. "What's the matter?"

Ty hesitated. "He's a talented horse, Amy."

"So? That's a good thing!" Amy frowned at his tone. "You make it sound like it's a problem."

"I think it is." Ty spoke quietly. He sighed. "I know you too well, Amy. You won't be happy riding a horse like Storm in local shows. It'll be fine at first, but then you'll want to do more — out-of-state shows, the winter circuit. How's Heartland going to fit into that?"

Amy stared. "We went through this yesterday. I told

you, I'm not going to let anything interfere with Heartland."

"So you're going to work nights and come home at lunch?" Ty said. "I don't think you'll be able to do it. But more than that, I don't even want to see you try. I don't want you to have to push yourself that hard."

'You're just trying to predict problems," Amy protested, running her fingers through Storm's mane all the while. "It'll work out — you'll see."

For a moment it looked as if Ty was going to argue some more, but then he shrugged. "OK, Amy. I'm sure you'll do what's best. And, just so you know, you and Storm look great together."

He gave her a slight smile and walked off.

Amy watched him go. It was obvious Ty wasn't convinced. But he was wrong. She would never neglect Heartland. She just wouldn't.

❧

"Nick Halliwell called while you were riding," Lou said as Amy washed her hands in the sink that evening. "He wants us to work with one of his young horses."

"Oh, yeah," Amy said, remembering the conversation she'd had with him at the Meadowville show. She looked across at Grandpa, sitting at the kitchen table. "He told me about it."

"I explained we're full at the moment," Lou said. She

had her car keys in her hand and looked as if she was about to go out. "But Nick doesn't want to send him anywhere else. Are any of the boarders ready to go home?"

"Maddison," Amy said. "He's loading just fine now. His owners could pick him up over the weekend."

"So Nick's horse could take that stall?"

"Sure," Amy said.

"Great," Lou said. "I'll call Nick tomorrow."

Amy headed for the stairs. "I'm going to get changed."

"Amy, before you go," Grandpa said, "we need to talk with you about something."

Amy walked slowly back to the table. She had a feeling she knew what he was going to say, and her throat suddenly felt dry.

Grandpa exchanged a look with Lou. "Lou and I were talking about going to the cemetery and having a reading," he said.

"OK . . . that sounds good," Amy stammered quickly.

"OK, I'm glad you agree. I'll —" But before Grandpa could finish his sentence, Amy had escaped up the stairs. Reaching her bedroom, she took a deep, trembling breath. The anniversary of her mom's death was less than three weeks away now. How was she ever going to get through it?

The sky was dark. A figure hurried through the driving rain toward the pickup. No! Amy tried to scream when she saw her mom open the driver's door, but no words came out. She couldn't speak, she couldn't move. As she sat beside her mom in the pickup, rainwater was flowing down the road. She was shivering and wet. The trailer behind them shook as the bay horse's hooves crashed into the metal sides, but the sound was immediately drowned out by a clap of thunder. A fork of lightning lit up the sky, and Amy started to scream. Then it happened. Straight in front of them, a tree started to fall. . . .

Amy awoke and sat up. She was trembling, sweating, afraid. It was that dream again. She hadn't had it for ages. Pushing back her damp hair, she flung her sheets back and walked shakily to the window. Early morning light was filtering through her curtains. Pulling them back, she opened the window and breathed in great gulps of the cool air.

As her heart slowed down, she glanced at her alarm clock. Almost six. She might as well get dressed and start on the barn chores. She certainly didn't want to go back to sleep again.

It was a lovely morning. The sun's rays were already glinting on the water in the trough. Storm was looking over his stall door, and he whinnied softly to her.

Changing her mind about starting the chores, Amy took Storm's saddle and bridle to his stall and tacked him up.

He nuzzled at her back as she was tightening the girth. She smiled. "Come on," she said. "Let's hit those trails."

It was the perfect morning for a ride, and as Amy trotted Storm along the sandy paths she felt the regular rhythm of his hoofbeats soothing her. By the time they got back to Heartland, her nightmares had vanished to the back of her mind.

Amy found it hard to concentrate on her classes in school that morning. She kept thinking about Storm. She imagined soaring over brightly colored jumps, the crowds in the grandstand cheering them on.

"So where's your head today?" Soraya said as they left the classroom at lunchtime.

"With Storm," Amy replied with a grin. "He's perfect, Soraya." She sighed. "I just wish Ty could see it. He seems so down on the idea of me taking him to shows."

Soraya shrugged. "Ty's not into showing. You know that. He doesn't get the whole competition thing."

"Yeah, I guess," Amy said. "I just can't believe he's being so negative about Storm. It's not like him."

"No," Soraya agreed. She looked thoughtful. "Maybe there's something else on his mind."

"Do you have any ideas?" Amy asked as they reached their lockers and started to put their books away.

Soraya hesitated. "Ty was pretty close to your mom, wasn't he? Maybe he's thinking about that — you know, since it was about this time . . ."

Amy felt her jaw tighten. "Maybe," she managed to say. "But he hasn't said anything."

Soraya looked at her. "You haven't exactly had a lot to say about it, either."

Amy froze.

"Amy, you haven't mentioned it at all," Soraya said quietly, her brown eyes scanning Amy's face. "It's not like you to keep things inside." When Amy didn't reply, Soraya sighed and continued to put her books away. "Look, I'm just saying that if you don't want to talk about it, don't be surprised if Ty doesn't, either."

Amy nodded. "I guess," she said forcing the words out.

Soraya touched her arm. "You know, I'm here if you need me," she said.

"Yeah, I know." Amy shut her locker door with a bang. "But I'm fine about it — just fine." She didn't want to discuss it — not even with Soraya. She fixed a smile on her face. "Come on. Let's go have lunch. I want to tell you about all the shows I've been thinking of for Storm."

✿

"There's a big improvement," Scott Trewin, the vet, said to Amy later that afternoon. He was examining Sundance's leg. "I'm pleased that the swelling's gone down so quickly."

"So what do we do now?" Amy asked.

"First, stop the cold treatment," Scott answered. "Then all he needs is lots of rest, and in a few days, you can start a little gentle exercise — not riding, just walking him by lead."

"Can he go out in the field?" Amy asked hopefully.

Scott shook his head. "I'm afraid not. If he canters around, he could damage the tendon again. That's the problem with injuries like this. The horse seems sound and feels better, but the tendon isn't fully repaired and is vulnerable to further injury."

"Will heat massage with oils help — and how about magnets?" Amy asked. "I was reading about them last night. This article suggested that magnetic boots can help healing."

"Heat massage is always a good idea," Scott replied. "And the magnetic boots are worth trying. You might be able to find some on the Internet. I'll check in on him in two weeks." They left Sundance and walked down the yard. "Is that your new horse?" Scott said, seeing Storm looking over his door.

"That's him," Amy said, going over.

"Any chance of seeing you ride him? Lou's been telling me that he's something special."

"Sure," Amy said eagerly. "I'm glad Lou said good things about him."

After tacking up Storm, Amy led him to the schooling ring and mounted. Ben had left a small course of four jumps out, and after warming up Storm she popped him over them.

The jumps were two-feet-six to three feet, and he cleared them effortlessly. Lou and Ben had joined Scott at the gate.

"Shall I raise the bars?" Ben called. "He's just stepping over them."

Amy paused. It was only the third time she'd ridden Storm, but jumping him just felt so natural — like they were a perfect team. "OK," she said.

Ben raised the jumps to just over four feet.

Her heart beating faster, Amy signaled Storm into a canter and then turned into the first jump. It loomed massively in front of her, but Storm soared over. A wide grin split Amy's face. He made the other three feel just as easy.

"What do you think?" Ben asked Scott as Amy rode over to them.

"He's got huge talent," Scott said.

Ben looked at Amy. "When are you going to start taking him to shows?"

"I haven't decided yet," she replied.

"I'm going to the East Creek show this weekend. It has a schooling ring where you can enter on the day," Ben said. "Why not come with me?"

"This weekend?" Amy echoed, thinking it was a bit soon.

"Why wait?" Scott shrugged. "He's jumping out of his skin. It would be a good experience for you both. And it's so close."

"OK," Amy said impulsively. "I will!"

Scott smiled at her. "Amy, the show jumper," he said. "Looks like it's not just your mom's gift of healing you've inherited. You've got her show-jumping talent, too."

Amy smiled as Scott's words echoed her thoughts from the day before. Could she really run Heartland and have a show-jumping career? Having Scott say it made it almost seem possible. Excitement flared inside her. If she did it, she'd be just like her mom. She patted Storm's neck. There was nothing she wanted more than that.

❧

The days before the show passed in a blur of activity, and almost before Amy knew it, Saturday arrived. At five o'clock in the morning, her alarm clock went off and she rolled out of bed, bleary-eyed and still half asleep.

"Maybe this show thing isn't such a good idea," she muttered to herself as she made coffee and headed out into the cool dawn to groom Storm.

Although it was only nine o'clock when she and Ben arrived at East Creek, the first classes had already started. Ben parked the trailer in the shade of some oak trees and then went off to check the jumping order while Amy unloaded Red and Storm. She looked around at the crowds and felt her excitement increase. She was riding at a show again — technically, she wasn't competing, but it was wonderful just to be there.

The schooling ring was set a little way off from the main rings. It had a course of eight jumps that could be adjusted to any height. After Amy had warmed up, she paid the steward. There were three other horses waiting to jump. While Amy waited her turn, she rode Storm around, half nervous, half excited. What was Storm going to be like?

"Is the height of the fences OK?" the steward asked when it was her turn.

The fences were about three feet nine — higher than she'd intended. She hesitated for a moment but then decided to go for it. "Fine." She nodded. "Thanks."

Taking a deep breath, she moved Storm into a canter and turned him into the first fence, a post and rails.

Storm's ears pricked, his stride lengthened, and he soared into the air.

In that moment, Amy's nerves vanished. When Storm landed, she felt like whooping with joy. This was where she belonged. This was what she should be doing. Her heart was pounding as she looked to the next fence, a red-and-white oxer. Storm met it with perfect timing.

The eight fences flowed by beneath them. When they landed over the last one, a happy smile broke across Amy's face.

"That was a great round," the steward said to her. "You looked like you were having a great time out there."

"I was!" Amy exclaimed, her eyes shining as she patted Storm's gray neck. Thanking the steward, she rode out of the ring.

"That was amazing!" Ben said.

"I know! Isn't he the best?" Amy said, jumping off and hugging Storm. But through her delight, she felt a faint flicker of disappointment as she realized that she'd already jumped her course and her moment at the show was over. She longed to be jumping Storm again. But the main classes had to be entered in advance.

One day, she said to herself, *we'll be going in classes and we'll be winning them all!*

Chapter Five

Amy and Ben walked Storm and Red back to the trailer. Storm's day was over, and Ben wanted to rest Red until his class. Leaving the two horses in the trailer, they headed off to explore the show ground. In the closest ring, the Modified Jumper was underway. The fences were set at four feet six, and any horses that went clear continued straight over the jump-off course, without leaving the ring. Amy knew that many of the riders in the Open Jumpers would use this class as a warm-up.

Amy and Ben bought a hot dog and Coke from one of the stalls and sat down to watch. The class was about halfway through.

"That was four faults for Helen Pierson on Boomerang. And now we have number 45, Daniel Lawson riding Burning Amber," the loudspeaker called.

Amy clutched Ben's arm. "It's that guy! The one I told you about. He's the one who won the Six Bar at Meadowville."

Ben watched as Amber trotted into the ring. "His horse isn't much of a looker, is it?"

"Wait till you see her jump," Amy said. "I bet she'll go clear."

Just as Amy had predicted, Amber jumped all eight fences of the first round without a fault, and then she tacked on a speedy clear for the shortened jump-off course. Still, Amy watched a bit skeptically. The roan mare had cleared the fences but hadn't jumped with the overwhelming willingness and desire that had made such an impression a week ago. Amy observed just the slightest hint of resistance — a swish of her tail as she approached the triple, her ears going back as she cleared the gate, a hesitation as she met the wall. But she had jumped clean, and that was the main thing. The crowd applauded as Daniel slowed her to a trot.

"You're right, they are good!" Ben said to Amy.

"Yeah," Amy said, but she spoke distractedly. She was puzzled at the change in the mare, and as Daniel rode out of the ring Amy was sure she saw a look of concern on his face.

However, the next horse quickly entered the ring, and Amy put Amber out of her mind.

When the class was finished, Ben stood up. "I'm going to get Red saddled up again," he said. "My class is next."

Amy went with him. As they walked past the in-gate they saw the seven riders who had placed come to the ring to collect their ribbons. Daniel was waiting to go in, his dark hair untidy, the reins looped over his arm. Amber was nuzzling his shoulder affectionately. He had won the class.

As Amy passed by, a glimmer of recognition crossed Daniel's face, and he scowled at her. Amy glared back and marched past.

While Ben worked Red, Amy stayed with Storm in case he became anxious without his stable companion. She needn't have worried. Storm was as calm as ever. Amy brushed him over and checked her watch. Ben should be going in soon. She'd better get going.

When she reached the ring, Ben was on deck. She wished him good luck and got a seat in the stands. The course of ten jumps was impressive — the fences were wide and solid and much more flashy and colorful than the schooling fences at Heartland. Ben trotted Red in.

Amy held her breath, particularly when Red nicked the top bar of the second jump with his back hoof. But it didn't fall, and Red cantered out with a clear round.

Ben was delighted. Leaving him to walk Red out, Amy decided to go back to the trailer to check on Storm.

As she headed for the trees, she saw a woman trying to load a palomino into a trailer. The horse, his ears back, was flatly refusing to step onto the ramp. The woman looked exhausted and impatient.

Amy stopped a little way off and watched. The woman tried bribing the horse with a bucket of food, trotting the horse toward the ramp, and using a crop to tap his flanks, but every time the horse stopped dead.

Seeing the woman start to look around in some desperation, Amy went over. "Do you want a hand?" she asked.

"Well, if you think you might have some luck with him," the woman said with a look of relief. "This is my first show, and I sure wasn't expecting him to behave like this."

Amy went to Ben's trailer and grabbed a bottle of diluted lavender oil from her grooming box. It was a great help in calming nervousness, and Amy always took it to shows.

Returning to the palomino, she rubbed a little of the oil on her hands. After taking off his lead rope, she began to massage it into his muzzle, speaking in soothing tones and avoiding eye contact with the horse to keep him from feeling threatened. That was when she noticed Daniel Lawson. He was standing a little way off under the trees, watching her curiously.

Amy turned her back on him and focused on the horse.

Twenty minutes later, after using the oil to calm the horse down and doing T-touch circles on his head and neck, Amy at last persuaded him to load.

"Thank you so much," his delighted owner said. "I don't know what you did, but I wouldn't have gotten him in without you."

"That's OK," Amy told her. "I'm just glad I could help."

Looking in through the side door, Amy said a quick good-bye to the palomino and then headed back to her own trailer.

"Hey!"

Amy turned around. It was Daniel Lawson, and he was coming toward her. Amy stiffened. What was he going to say now? She didn't want another confrontation. But the scowl had left his face. He jogged up to her, his brown eyes lighted up.

"How did you do that?" he asked as he stopped in front of her. "I watched the whole thing. That horse was absolutely defiant. Then you just seemed to rub its neck and face. And presto!"

Amy hesitated, but he looked genuinely intrigued. "I was doing something called T-touch," she replied. "It builds up trust with a horse by helping to relieve tension.

We use it a lot at my family's farm." Daniel continued to look at her, so Amy continued. "We have a horse sanctuary called Heartland. We help damaged horses there, healing and rehoming them."

Daniel stared curiously at her. "Really?"

When Amy nodded, he shook his head. "I'm sorry about last weekend. I had you all wrong," he said. "I thought you were just a typical stuck-up show type, in it for the gossip. But now it seems you're not like that at all."

"Of course I'm not," Amy protested, unconsciously folding her arms. "Why would you think I was?"

Daniel's eyes narrowed. "I saw you and your friend laughing at Amber. I mean, I know she's not the most beautiful horse, but she is wonderful and she sure can jump. I get really defensive when people treat her like she's a joke."

"Me and my friend laughing?" Amy said, thinking back and wondering what he was talking about. She and Hannah certainly hadn't laughed at Amber.

"Yeah, that blond girl on the dainty chestnut."

"Chestnut?" Amy said, surprised. Her eyes widened as she suddenly realized who he was talking about. "You mean Ashley? I wouldn't call her a friend!"

Daniel stared. "But you were talking."

"Arguing, more like," Amy said. She shook her head indignantly. "I'd never laugh at any horse, no matter what it looked like."

Daniel looked genuinely taken aback. "Oh." He bit his lip. "I had you down as someone who wouldn't look at a horse that didn't have the right pedigree. Someone with a horse that cost more than five figures."

Amy started to deny it, but all of a sudden she felt uncomfortably aware of Storm — of the fact that he was an imported horse with a fine record and probably an impressive price tag. She quickly swallowed that thought and changed the subject.

"The friend I was with, Hannah Boswell, said that you bought Amber at a horse sale," Amy said.

Daniel nodded. "I work for a dealer south of here, and he sent me to look out for a couple of pleasure horses. I saw Amber there. She was really thin, and no one wanted her." He hesitated, as if wondering how much more to say.

"We got Sundance like that," Amy said. "He's my pony. He was going to go for meat because he had such a bad attitude, but I persuaded Mom to buy him."

"Really?"

When Amy nodded, Daniel said, "Everyone at the sale was laughing at Amber as they walked by her pen. I had to buy her. I had some money that I was saving to buy a show jumper, so I used that." He smiled at the memory. "I never thought Amber would turn out to be that show jumper."

"Is that what you want to do?" Amy asked. "On a professional level?"

"It's all I've ever wanted to do," Daniel said. "But my dad . . ." He swallowed. "Well, he was never going to buy me a horse, so I always knew I'd have to do it on my own."

"Who is the dealer you work for? Is he into jumping?" Amy asked.

Daniel shook his head. "Not really. I want to get a place as a working pupil at a show-jumping barn. That's why I've started traveling up here to compete. Brad Shaffer saw me in the Six Bar last week, and he agreed to put me on his list of potential working pupils."

"Brad Shaffer! That's great!" Amy said. He was the leading show jumper in Maryland. Positions at barns like his were as good as gold.

Daniel nodded. "All the people he's considering have been asked to compete at a show in Maryland next weekend," he said. "Brad says that he'll make his selection after that."

"You'll do well," Amy said, finding herself wishing Daniel the very best now that she knew his story. "You and Amber are just amazing."

"Well, Amber is a star," Daniel said slowly. "Except when she gets grumpy."

"Amy!"

Amy swung around. Ben was riding toward her. Amy's hand flew to her mouth. The jump-off! She'd forgotten all about it.

"I'm really sorry!" she gasped. "I was helping some-one load a horse, and then . . ." She broke off as she caught sight of a blue ribbon fluttering on Red's bridle. "You won!"

"Yeah. Red was great!" Ben grinned, swinging his leg over the saddle and dismounting.

"I wish I'd been there to watch," Amy said. "I'm glad Red's back to his old self."

"He is," Ben said, patting his horse. "He was fabulous. A clear round, and he was three seconds faster than everyone else."

Amy stroked the chestnut's nose. "Smart boy."

She saw Ben glance at Daniel.

"This is Daniel," Amy said quickly. "Do you remember — we saw him in the ring? Daniel, this is my friend Ben."

Daniel nodded at Ben. "I'd better go," he said shortly. "It was good to talk to you, Amy. Are you here tomor-row?"

"I'm not sure," Amy said. She knew Ben was entered in another Intermediate class the next day and she was tempted to come back and cheer him on.

"Well, if you are, I might catch you then," Daniel said. "I'm in the Open." He gave her a quick smile and walked off.

Ben looked at Amy in astonishment. She didn't blame him. After all, just a few hours ago she'd been recount-ing how rude Daniel had been.

"We started talking," she said, explaining. "After I loaded the horse." They started to walk back to the trailer. "He was telling me about how he wants to be a show jumper and how he bought Amber at a horse sale when no one else wanted her."

Ben looked at her slyly. "I think he likes you."

"What? Daniel?" Amy stared. "No way."

"Are you sure?" he asked. "Amy, look for me, *I'm in the Open,*" Ben teased in a mocking voice.

"Come on, Ben. Don't be ridiculous," Amy said, meaning it. She'd sensed a connection with Daniel when they'd talked about Amber and his show jumping, but that had been all. "I think he was just glad to talk to someone who wasn't going to laugh at Amber," she told Ben. "From what he was saying, I don't think he has many friends on the circuit."

Ben nodded. "It's lonely going to shows on your own," he said when they reached the trailer. "It's been much better for me having you here." He looked at her mischievously. "Even if you did miss the jump-off."

"Oh, I'm so sorry," Amy said.

"You can make it up to me by coming back tomorrow," Ben said. He saw her start to shake her head.

"I've got so much to do at home," she said.

"My class is first thing," he told her. "We can be back by eleven. It would be good to have your support."

Amy hesitated. They could be back at Heartland by

lunchtime, and she did want to see Ben ride again. "OK, it's a deal," she said. "I'll come."

❧

They got back to Heartland just after lunch. When Ty came down the yard to meet them, Ben told him about Amy's clear round and his own first place.

"That's good," Ty said. Not asking anything more, he started to help Ben lower the ramp.

"What's been going on here?" Amy asked as she untied Storm and led him out of the trailer.

"Just the usual," Ty replied. "Mrs. Hampton called and said she's coming to pick up Maddison about four, so I called Nick Halliwell to let him know that a stall's going to be empty. His pickup is in the shop so he asked if we could go and get the horse, Dylan, either tomorrow or Monday. It'll be quite a drive now that he's moved to his new farm, but I said that it would be fine. I've got to call him back and tell him when. I thought tomorrow."

"No, Monday," Amy said, without thinking. "I'm going to the show with Ben again tomorrow."

"Well, OK." Ty stiffened. "I guess if you're going to a show, then it'll have to be Monday."

Amy could tell she'd annoyed him and quickly tried to make things better. "Look, we can still go tomorrow. Ben and I won't be at the show for long. His class is the first one. We could go to Nick's in the afternoon."

"Forget it, Amy," Ty said, picking up the saddles. "It can't happen tomorrow if you're out until the afternoon. There'll be other things to do. There are always other things to do."

"Ty, that's not fair. We can do it, I'm sure," Amy protested in surprise.

But Ty was already walking away.

Amy's heart sank. She hated arguing with Ty, but she wasn't going to give up going to shows just to please him. She could compete Storm and still do just as much at Heartland, she knew she could.

She sighed. The problem was — how could she convince Ty?

Chapter Six

"That was great!" Amy called as Ben trotted Red out of the showring the following day.

Ben halted Red, a wide smile on his face. "He's never jumped this well."

"You're a star, aren't you, boy?" Amy said, stroking the big chestnut. "And I bet you're going to win."

"It depends how fast the others go," Ben said, dismounting.

Unlike the day before, any competitor who went clear in the Intermediate immediately did the jump-off course. Having completed the jump-off course with no faults and a fast time, Red was now leading the class. But there were still six horses to go.

"I'll cool him down if you want to watch the rest of riders," Amy suggested.

"Thanks," Ben said gratefully. He gave Red a pat and headed for the stands.

As Amy led him past the warm-up ring, she saw Daniel schooling Amber. Amy waved, but Daniel was concentrating and didn't see her. Amber wasn't going well. Her head was up and her back was hollow.

Amy stopped Red for a moment to watch. Daniel sat deep in the saddle and signaled Amber to canter. The roan mare swished her tail and threw her head back. Daniel pushed her again, and with an angry half buck, Amber obeyed.

Amy frowned. What was the matter? She remembered Daniel's words from the day before. He'd said that Amber was sometimes grumpy. Was this what he'd meant? Amy could see why Daniel looked so worried, especially if Brad Shaffer was going to be picking his pupil next week.

Amber's strides continued to be stilted. Daniel turned into the practice fence.

Amber jumped flat and sent the top poles flying. Daniel halted her near the center of the ring, took a deep breath, and looked up.

Amy lifted her hand in greeting.

Giving Amber her head, Daniel rode over to the fence on a loose rein. "Going well, isn't she?" he joked, but Amy could see that there was no laughter in his eyes.

"What's up?" Amy said as Red reached forward to

touch noses with Amber. The roan mare squealed and threw her head back.

"It's just one of her moods," Daniel said, frowning. "Amber gets like this just before she goes into heat. She's really irritable and won't jump. The vet thinks it's a hormonal imbalance."

Amy remembered mares coming to Heartland that had similar problems. "But surely you can treat it," she said.

Daniel nodded. "The vet put her on some hormone powders that made her calmer, but you can't use them for long because it can be bad for the horse, and" — he looked awkward — "well, they're expensive, and I really can't afford them. I just manage to compete as it is, and I'm trying to save for a new trailer, so I thought I'd just do without them. It's been OK until now. I've always withdrawn from shows when she's been like this, but if I pull out of next weekend I'll never get the position at Brad's."

"Can't you just get a treatment for this week?" Amy asked.

Daniel shook his head. "You have to give them at the right point in the mare's cycle, before she starts acting up."

Amy thought quickly. "I bet you can treat the problem with herbs," she said.

"But don't herbal medicines take ages to work?"

Daniel said. "They wouldn't make her better for next weekend."

He was right. Generally, natural therapies didn't have an immediate effect on a problem. "It's worth a try, though," Amy told him. "Give me your phone number, and I'll call you when I get back to Heartland and find out what you need."

"All right," Daniel said, not looking totally convinced. "Thanks." Resignedly, he patted Amber's neck. "Well, I guess I'd better scratch my class. There's no point in trying to compete when she's like this. Talk to you later?"

"Sure," Amy replied.

Amy led Red for a while longer and then took him back to the Jumper ring. She wondered if Red was still in the lead.

A horse came cantering out of the ring to polite applause. "That's four faults for number 63, Jennifer Rosen on Going for a Song," the loudspeaker crackled. "And that concludes the Intermediate Jumper."

Amy searched the stands and found Ben. He was hurrying toward her.

"We placed second!" he told her.

"That's great!" Amy cried in delight.

Quickly, Ben tightened the girth and mounted. The

prizewinners were being called into the ring. Red looked handsome when Ben rode up to collect his red rosette. Amy clapped as loudly as she could. With the first place finish from the day before, Red also received a sash and ribbon for being the Intermediate Champion. Amy was as thrilled as if she had earned the award herself. Ben had worked so hard with Red, and it was wonderful to see him winning now.

They drove home from the show with the ribbons proudly attached to the inside of the windshield. *Someday, Storm will win ribbons and trophies,* Amy thought to herself.

❧

Amy remembered her promise to Daniel, and the moment they got back to Heartland she went to the tack room to check the books. The sooner Daniel knew what herb he needed, the sooner he could start treating Amber. In her mom's notes she read:

Mares with behavioral problems due to hormonal fluctuations: *Clinical tests suggest that the herb* Agnus castus *can be effective in such cases. It appears to interact with the hormonal balance, gently helping the body to self-correct. N.B.* Agnus castus *works gradually and does not usually bring about an immediate change in a mare's behavior.*

Amy sighed. It was just as Daniel had thought. But then she saw that her mom had made a note in the margin.

Have had luck with it working quickly — occasionally in a few days.

Amy skimmed the rest of the notes. They suggested feeding fifteen grams daily, split between two feeds. It wasn't to be used with pregnant mares, but other than that it was considered safe, with no complications. She turned the page. At the end of the section, her mom had made another note.

Not easy to find locally. Contact growers for own supply. Collect seeds and fruit in autumn, freeze or dry for storage.

Amy checked the cupboard in the feed room. Ty kept it well stocked, harvesting herbs at the appropriate times throughout the year and storing them. Amy found a half bottle of dried *Agnus castus*.

She called Daniel's cell phone.

"Hi, it's Amy Fleming," she said when he answered. She told him what she had discovered. "I found some information on hormonal imbalances. It looks like *Agnus castus* is the herb you want. It can work fast — so it's worth a try."

"Really?" Daniel said, sounding brighter. "That's good news."

"The only problem is," Amy continued, "it's difficult to get hold of. We have half a bottle here at Heartland. If you want you can drive over and pick it up before you go home."

"I've already left the show," Daniel said. "I didn't see any point in hanging around. But don't worry, I'm sure I'll be able to get hold of some over the Internet."

"But then you'll have to wait for it to arrive," Amy replied. "And you need to start it as soon as possible if you're going to have any chance of it working by the weekend. It'll take at least three days." An idea came to her. "Where do you live?"

"Just north of Lexington," Daniel answered.

"I know what we can do," Amy said. "Ty and I are heading your way tomorrow — we're getting a horse from Nick Halliwell's near Charlottesville. We could stop by on the way there."

"I can't let you do that," Daniel protested. "It's miles out of your way."

"It's no problem," Amy said. "Now, where do you live?"

Sounding reluctant, Daniel gave her his address. "Look, if it becomes a problem, I'll understand, and I'll just call the stores in my area to see if any of them have it in stock."

"It's Memorial Day tomorrow — they'll probably be closed," Amy reminded him. "Even more reason for us to come. We'll see you about two o'clock."

She replaced the receiver. As she left the kitchen, she saw Ty leading Solo down the yard.

"Ty!" Excited by the thought of helping Daniel and Amber, Amy ran across the gravel driveway toward him. "Tomorrow, when we go for Dylan, we need to make a stop in Lexington as well. There's this guy, Daniel, we've got to help him. He's . . ."

"OK. Slow down." Ty interrupted her, halting Solo. "Now tell me — why do we have to go to Lexington tomorrow?"

"I told you about Daniel," Amy tried to explain. "We met at Meadowville where he won the Six Bar." She explained about him needing the *Agnus castus* before the next weekend. "I said we could drop some off tomorrow when we go to Nick's."

Ty stared at her incredulously. "But Lexington is at least an hour from there. You said we'd go all that way just to give this guy an herb so he can go to a show? Amy, have you gone crazy?"

"You don't understand," Amy protested. "He really needs it. It might help Amber get back on track."

Ty shook his head. "Don't you think we have better things to do than run all over the state so you can do a favor for one of your show friends?" He continued to lead Solo toward his stall.

"Ty!" Amy almost shouted in exasperation. "You don't understand. It's not just any show for Daniel and Amber. It's their future."

Ty stopped and raised his eyebrows skeptically, responding to her desperate tone.

"Daniel doesn't have much money. He's really worked hard to get to where he is," Amy explained quickly before he could speak. "Now he's been offered the chance to compete for a working pupil position at Brad Shaffer's stable, and the show is next weekend." Her eyes pleaded with Ty to understand. "I just want to help."

She saw some of the tension leave Ty's face. "Well, I guess it is a pretty big opportunity for them," he said.

"Please, Ty," Amy said, encouraged. "He's a nice guy, and he deserves to have a fair chance. He rescued Amber when no one else wanted her. You'd like him."

Ty didn't look convinced. "I don't know how you always get yourself into these things, but all right," he said reluctantly. "We can go."

Amy's breath left her in a rush. "Thank you," she said. Impulsively, she hugged him.

Ty's free arm folded around her, but he let go when Solo pulled on the lead, stretching his neck toward a tall tuft of grass. As Ty redirected his attention to the horse,

Amy became aware of his doubt. She realized that, although he might have agreed to go to Daniel's, he still had his reservations.

She stepped toward him, hoping to explain. "Ty, don't be angry with me."

His eyebrows immediately creased into a scowl. "I don't know what you're talking about," he said and, clicking his tongue, he led Solo into his stall.

For a moment, Amy wondered whether to let it go, but she couldn't. "Ty, that's not true," she said, following him. "I know you think that if I start going to shows I'll neglect our work at Heartland. But I've told you that won't happen. I took care of all my work yesterday even though I went to a show, and I'll do the same today. I'll find time for everything."

Ty stopped in the middle of unsaddling Solo. "Amy, there's so much to do. There's no way to get to *everything*."

"What do you mean?" Amy demanded. "What did I miss?"

"Well, for one thing," Ty said, "I haven't seen you take the time to help Lou start to ride again. You know she won't do it on her own."

Amy stared at him. He was right. She'd been so busy over the last few days that she'd totally forgotten about Lou. It *was* something she wanted to do.

"See what I mean?" Ty said quietly. "There's no way

to do it all." Picking up Solo's saddle and bridle, he left the stall.

Slowly, Amy walked over to where Storm was looking out over his half door. He nuzzled her hair but she hardly noticed. How could she have forgotten Lou? And she'd thought she'd been coping so well — getting everything done, fitting it all in. Storm had only been here a week, and she was already getting behind.

She made up her mind. She'd been going to brush Storm over, but he could wait.

"I'll groom you later, boy," she said. "Right now, there's something I've got to do."

Giving him a pat, she hurried to the house.

Lou was in the office. She looked up when Amy opened the door. "Hi. How did Ben do at the show?"

"Really well," Amy said. "He placed second, and Red was Champion." But she didn't want to talk about the show. "Lou, I was wondering. Would — would you like to ride Dancer this afternoon?"

Lou looked startled. "Ride? This afternoon?"

"Dancer's very quiet," Amy said quickly. "I should have asked you before, but I've been so busy I kind of forgot. I'm sorry."

"It's all right — I know how crazy it's been," Lou said. She played with the pen she was holding.

Amy nodded. "Dancer's a sweetheart," Amy continued before Lou had a chance to answer. She looked carefully at her sister's anxious face. "You'd enjoy riding her, and she needs a light workout."

Lou hesitated.

"Come on, Lou," Amy pleaded. "You said you wanted to start riding again. Why not now — today?"

A mixture of emotions reflected in Lou's blue eyes — apprehension and fear, but also determination and pride. She nodded slowly. "OK, I will."

Amy was delighted. "You'll be so happy when you're done!"

Lou looked nervous. "I hope so," she said.

Chapter Seven

❧

"Well, here goes. Wish me luck." Lou gathered Dancer's reins and put her left foot in the stirrup. But just as she seemed about to mount, she stopped.

Amy saw the fear in her sister's eyes. "You'll be fine," she said reassuringly. "Dancer's really calm."

Lou still hesitated.

"You can do it, Lou," Amy said.

A look of determination crossed Lou's face. "Yes," she said positively. "I can."

Putting her right hand on the saddle again, she hopped on her foot twice and swung herself up. After she landed, she clutched nervously at the reins and dug her knees tight into Dancer's sides.

"Dancer's not going to do anything," Amy said. "You can loosen your hold."

Very slowly, Lou let out her reins. With a trembling hand, she patted Dancer's brown-and-white neck.

"We won't do anything until you're ready," Amy said.

They stood there until, gradually, Lou started to relax. "I think I'm ready to walk," she said at last.

With Amy walking beside Dancer, they set off around the ring. At first Lou sat stiffly in the saddle and let Amy direct Dancer. But after a few circuits, she began to use her legs and hands to guide the horse herself.

"I'll stand here now," Amy said, stopping in the middle, judging that her sister was now confident enough to ride on her own. Lou rode Dancer slowly around the ring.

"I think I might try a trot," she said after a few minutes.

"Good idea," Amy called.

Dancer listened and moved forward into a trot. Lou's lower legs were a little wobbly, and her hands jerked on the reins as she tried to follow Dancer's movements. But gradually, she found her balance and the posting rhythm. *She's doing just fine,* Amy thought, feeling pleased.

Lou fixed her grip on the reins. With every circuit, she looked more confident. And by the time she brought Dancer to a halt, she was actually smiling.

"Are you going to try to canter?" Amy asked.

"Not yet," Lou said. "Maybe next time."

"So, there's going to be a next time?" Amy said happily.

"Definitely," Lou answered, patting Dancer's neck.

"I'd forgotten how good riding feels." She dismounted, smiling. "I didn't do much, but I really had a good time. Thanks, Amy."

Amy looked at her teasingly. "You wait. You'll be jumping soon."

Lou grinned back. "We'll see."

Lou helped Amy untack Dancer, and together they went down to the tack room, where they found Ty cleaning a bridle. "Had a good time?" he asked as they came in.

"I really enjoyed myself," Lou said, glancing at Amy gratefully. "And it's all because of Amy. If she hadn't put me up to it I'd still be sitting in the office at the computer."

Amy couldn't meet Ty's eyes, she was so embarrassed. After all, he knew exactly what had prompted her to go and find Lou and make her ride this afternoon. "I'd better get on with things," she said, shoving Dancer's bridle on its peg and hurrying back to the yard.

Amy avoided Ty for the rest of the afternoon. She was starting to feel awkward when she was around him. It wasn't just that she felt embarrassed about Lou, it was also difficult not mentioning Storm or shows in case he got upset. She was so used to being able to tell him everything that it was really hard to have things they couldn't talk about.

The next morning, Amy found the *Agnus castus* and made her way to the trailer, where Ty was waiting for her. As she walked down the yard, Amy realized that she was dreading the journey ahead. What would they talk about on such a long drive?

She got into the pickup and shot a quick look at Ty. He put the keys into the ignition, his face unreadable. "Have you got everything?" he asked.

Amy nodded.

"Let's go then," Ty said briefly.

They drove out of Heartland in silence. Amy stared out the window, feeling tense. It was as if an invisible barrier had gone up between them, and she hated it.

Feeling miserable, she glanced at Ty. He was looking at her. For a moment, she thought he was going to say something. But then he seemed to change his mind. He turned his attention back to driving, and the silence continued, broken only by the monotonous rattles and groans from the engine.

❧

Just before two o'clock, Amy and Ty arrived at North Run, the dealer's barn where Daniel worked. A weatherboarded house, a schooling ring, and two barns with red walls and white roofs stood at the end of a driveway. Amy read a wooden sign by the path that led to the barns: JEFF CLARK. QUALITY HORSES BOUGHT AND SOLD.

A red-haired man came out of the nearest barn. "Hi," he said, smiling at them. "Can I help you?"

"We're here to see Daniel," Amy said.

The man's smile faded. "I'll get him." He turned, but Daniel was already coming out of the other barn.

"Amy!" Daniel called, jogging over. He turned to the man. "Jeff, this is a friend of mine. I'll take my lunch break now if that's OK."

Jeff nodded brusquely. "Just remember, we've got a client coming in half an hour," he said, striding back into the barn.

"My boss," Daniel said to Amy. "He's in a bad mood because I was at the show for the last two days." He looked at Ty.

"This is Ty," Amy said. "We work together at Heartland. Ty, this is Daniel."

Daniel and Ty nodded at each other. Amy saw the reservation in both their eyes, and her heart sank. She really wanted Ty to understand why she wanted to help Daniel.

"So," she said, speaking quickly to make up for the fact that they weren't saying anything, "where's Amber? Which is her stall?"

"It's in the left barn, but she only goes into it in really bad weather," Daniel answered. "I think she may have had a bad experience in a stall before I got her. She gets really stressed out and doesn't eat if she's stuck in there for too long. I keep her out in the field most of the time. It's a nightmare in the winter because I obviously can't have her fully clipped — she'd just get too cold. But I'd rather have the extra work grooming her heavy coat than have her cold or unhappy."

He led them around to a field at the back of the barns. Amber was grazing, swishing her tail at the flies. Her ears were back and she didn't look happy. Daniel called her name. The change in the mare was immediate. She looked up and whinnied loudly. Then, pricking her ears, she came trotting over.

Daniel climbed over the gate and went to meet her. Amber stopped in front of him and rubbed her heavy, straight-nosed head against his chest, half closing her small eyes in enjoyment as he scratched her forehead.

"How's she been?" Amy asked Daniel.

"Same as she usually is when she gets in these moods," he replied. "She's fine when I handle her in the field, but as soon as I try to ride she gets irritable."

"Well, I've got the *Agnus castus*," Amy said, holding up the bottle. "You need to give her fifteen milligrams a day. Split it between two feeds."

"Thanks," Daniel said gratefully. "I hope it works."

Ty had walked to the fence and was looking at Amber. "Can I check her over?"

Daniel looked unsure. "She may try to bite. She's not

crazy about strangers when she's like this. But be my guest." He led her nearer.

"Hey there, girl," Ty murmured, climbing over the gate and approaching Amber. She swung her teeth at him, but Ty stood his ground. He stroked her neck, and then his fingers began to move in T-touch circles. As his hands worked their way up Amber's neck, Amy saw the mare begin to relax.

"That's what you did, isn't it?" Daniel said as he joined her at the gate. "With that horse at the show?"

Amy nodded.

She and Daniel watched Ty's skillful fingers move up to the mare's head, instinctively finding the right places to work. As he worked around her temples and fore-head, she sighed deeply.

Amy looked at Daniel and saw that he was looking very surprised. "She won't normally let anyone but me touch her when she's like this," he said.

"She's not herself, is she?" Ty said softly, his eyes on the mare. "She feels tense. In addition to the *Agnus cas-tus*, I'd try giving her Impatiens — it's a Bach Flower Remedy. It should help reduce her irritability and ten-sion."

"OK," Daniel said. "Anything's worth a try." He smiled at Ty for the first time. "Thanks."

"No problem," Ty said. He stepped back from the

mare, and to Amy's relief, she saw that he, too, had re-laxed. "Amy told me you've got a big show next weekend."

Daniel nodded and explained about the working pupil place he was trying to get. "It's hard to get accepted at a place like Brad's," he said. "But it's the only way I'm ever going to get to the top. Jeff can't give me the time off to compete as much as I need to, and I don't make enough to compete seriously. There are just too many shows."

"How long have you worked for Jeff?" Amy asked.

"Full-time since I was sixteen," Daniel answered. "But I began helping out when I was twelve. I wasn't into horses then, but I needed the money and Jeff wanted help with the mucking out on weekends. I started riding because I was here. Jeff didn't have anyone light enough to exercise the smaller ponies, so he put me up on them." He shrugged. "My riding improved, and I started taking them in shows for Jeff. Then I moved on to the horses. When I was old enough to leave school, Jeff offered me an on-site job. I sleep in a trailer in back of the house and keep an eye on the barns." He seemed to remember his manners. "Would you like a drink?"

"Thanks," Amy said.

She and Ty followed Daniel to his trailer.

"Not much, is it?" Daniel said, looking around at the bare green walls and old brown sofa.

He carried three glasses of lemonade out, and they sat on the grass.

"So when did you get Amber?" Ty asked.

Daniel explained about the horse sale. "At first I thought I was crazy — I'd been saving the money to buy a hunter. A sleek, young, green horse. Amber couldn't have been further from what I'd imagined. But something told me that she needed me. It was the best thing I ever did. She's amazing."

Amy nodded. "You should see her jump, Ty. That time I saw you at Meadowville," she said to Daniel, "you and Amber just seemed to have this bond between you. She was so smart and willing — she looked like she'd jump over the moon for you."

Daniel smiled. "She might not be a Thoroughbred, but she's tough and brave and has a bigger heart than any other horse I've ever ridden."

"What about your parents?" Amy asked. "Do they come and watch you?"

The softness that had been in Daniel's eyes vanished. "My parents?" he said, his voice suddenly icy. "They don't even know where I live."

Amy stared. "Why?"

"My mom left when I was eight. I haven't seen her since then. I grew up with my dad in a trailer park. And he — well," — Daniel looked out over the fields — "all he cares about is having a bottle in his hand."

Neither Amy nor Ty spoke. It was hard to think of anything to say.

"So that's my life," Daniel said in a hard voice. "And this is my home." He looked at Amy. "That working pupil post is the only way out."

She nodded. "Would you miss this place — and Jeff?"

"There's not much to miss," Daniel confided. "Don't start to think that Jeff's been some sort of mentor or father figure. As long as I work fourteen-hour days and don't complain, he's happy. He's my boss. There's never been more than a paycheck between us."

"Daniel!"

Hearing the angry shout, they all looked around. Jeff was walking toward them. "I told you we've got a client coming," he said. "The horses aren't even tacked up yet! Get a move on!" He glared at Daniel, Amy, and Ty and then marched back down the path.

Daniel got to his feet. "I'd better go," he said. "I feel bad. You've come all this way, but . . ."

"Don't worry," Amy said quickly, getting up. "We understand."

"It's been good to meet you, Daniel," Ty said. "I sure hope the *Agnus* works."

"Thanks," Daniel said. He looked at Amy. "Are you going to be at the show?"

Amy felt awkward, aware of what Ty would say if she went to another show so soon. "No," she said. She saw Daniel's face fall. "We've got a lot going on at the moment," she tried to explain. "It's difficult."

Daniel nodded understandingly. "Well, I'll let you know how it goes. See you."

☞

Amy and Ty went back to the pickup. As Ty started the engine, Amy looked across at him, wanting to ask if he liked Daniel, but the question died on her lips. Ty looked lost in thought, staring out the windshield.

"What's up?" Amy asked.

"That could have been me," Ty said quietly.

"What do you mean?" Amy said, looking at him in surprise.

Ty shook his head. "I could have ended up in a place like this." He saw the confusion on Amy's face. "Don't you see?" he said. "Daniel and I are alike. We have so much in common. Neither of us has a horse background. We both started working with horses because we needed the money, and now we're both doing it as a career. OK, I haven't had it anywhere near as tough as Daniel. My dad might not care about what I do, but at least he doesn't drink. And my mom might not be well, but at least she's still around. But our stories are similar, and if I hadn't met your mom, I could have been just like him — living in a trailer, putting in the hours for a boss like Jeff." He shook his head. "When you first told me about Daniel, I thought he was just part of the show scene, and I didn't get why he needed our help, why he was worth the time."

"I just thought he deserved a break," Amy said. "I mean, nothing's been easy for him."

"I understand that now," Ty nodded. "Seeing him makes me realize how much I owe your mom. She believed in me when no one else did." He shook his head. "Marion was so important to me. She made me feel like I was important. I can't believe it's a year since . . ." His voice trailed off. He sighed. "Look, I'm sorry. I didn't mean to bring it up. But the fact that it's almost a year has really been on my mind."

"It's OK," Amy said. "I understand." She took a deep breath. "Grandpa wants Lou and me to go to the cemetery on the anniversary. Do you think you could come?"

"You know I will," Ty answered. He looked at her sympathetically. "How are you holding up?"

Amy shrugged and stared at her knees.

To her relief, Ty didn't push it. "It's OK," he said softly. "It's hard for me, too." With that, he released the parking brake and pulled back onto the road. Amy watched out the sideview mirror as the riding farm disappeared in the distance.

When they reached Nick's barn they were greeted by Taylor Ellis, the head groom. He showed them the horse they were to take back to Heartland. Dylan was tall, a light bay of about seventeen hands. They watched Taylor riding him. The gangly bay was fine on a loose rein, but as soon as Taylor asked him to collect, he started to resist. When Taylor tried to trot over some ground poles, Dylan threw his head up, tripped over the first pole, and then bolted off to the side in a panic.

"He does it every time. I've never seen a horse act this way before," Taylor said as he brought Dylan to a stop.

"Has he been checked out by a vet?" Ty asked.

Taylor nodded. "Our vet says he's fine. There doesn't seem to be anything physically wrong."

Amy patted the bay. "Well, we'll see what we can do."

Taylor dismounted. "Come on, Dylan, let's get you ready for the road."

When the horse's legs were wrapped, Taylor led him into the Heartland trailer. As they walked up the ramp together, the bay stepped on Taylor's foot with one of his hooves.

Taylor yelled in pain, and he shoved Dylan along the chest to get him to move his leg.

"You OK?" Amy asked in concern.

Taylor grimaced. "I'll live." He frowned at Dylan. "He's the clumsiest creature on this earth. He's always stepping on people and knocking them over. I don't know how we'll make a jumper out of him."

Amy frowned. "Did the vet test his eyes?"

Taylor nodded. "His vision's fine. He just doesn't seem to know where he's putting his hooves!" He tied Dylan up inside and then helped haul up the ramp. "Good luck with him!" he said. "You'll need it!"

❧

"What do you think's the matter?" Amy asked when they reached the highway and headed back to Heartland.

"I don't know," Ty replied thoughtfully. "But I've never seen anything like that — the way he shied away from those poles. At least Mercury outright refused them. This is something different."

Amy nodded, remembering the challenge they had faced in getting Mercury to start jumping again. For Mercury, it was a psychological obstacle. Ty was right, it seemed different with Dylan. She pictured Dylan going over the cavellettis. He had looked panicked as he had trotted over them, his legs going in all directions. "It was almost like he didn't know where he was putting his feet," she said slowly. "His hooves just seemed to go everywhere, and . . ."

"Amy, that's it!" Ty exclaimed. "He doesn't know where he's putting his feet! I remember reading about it in your mom's book on T-touch. It said it's not that uncommon for horses to have trouble knowing where their own feet are. So when they're asked to do things that take lots of coordination — like working on a tight rein or going over poles — they find it really hard and can even get tense and defensive. Sounds like Dylan to me!"

"It makes sense," Amy said as she suddenly remembered reading the same thing. "The book said to use T-touch because it helps a horse become more aware of the different parts of its body."

"Once he's more aware, we can do ground exercises, too," Ty said. "If we put together a maze of poles for him to work his way through, he'll build up his coordination and confidence."

Amy looked at Ty in delight. "I think we've got it. I'm sure this is the way to help Dylan!"

Their gazes met. In Ty's eyes, Amy could see the same enthusiasm she was feeling. They couldn't wait to get to work.

Chapter Eight

When Amy got home from school the next day, Daniel phoned.

"Hey," Amy said. "How's Amber doing?"

"I don't know if it's because of that stuff you gave me," Daniel said, "but she sure seems calmer."

"Maybe it's helping," Amy said optimistically.

"I hope so," Daniel said. "It's only four days to the show. Brad called earlier to make sure I was still going."

"You said you were, didn't you?" Amy asked.

"Yes." She heard Daniel hesitate. "Are you sure you can't come and watch? It can't be that far from you."

"It's not," Amy said. "But we're so busy right now. I really wish I could be there. Will you call me and tell me how it goes?"

"Of course," Daniel replied. "Especially if we go clear and Brad offers me the position."

As Amy went outside, she thought about the show. She wanted to go, but there was so much to do at Heartland, and she had spent most of the previous weekend at a show.

Ty was scrubbing the feed buckets by the tap.

"Daniel just called," Amy said as she approached him. "Amber seems a little more relaxed."

Ty straightened up. "That's good. She'll probably get even better as the herb builds up in her system." He dried his hands on his jeans. "Look, I've been thinking," he said slowly. "I guess Daniel would really like you to go to this show, wouldn't he?"

Hope leaped into Amy's eyes. Where was this leading? "I think he would," she told him.

"Well, you should go then," Ty said. "I think he could use the support. Ben and I can manage here for a day."

"Are you sure?" Amy asked quickly.

Ty nodded.

"Oh, Ty." Amy stepped forward and wrapped her arms around his back. She knew how much it meant for him to have suggested such a thing. It was his way of saying sorry, his way of saying that helping Daniel was important. Amy gave Ty a quick hug and pulled away to look into his eyes. "Thank you," she said.

❧

Amy flew through her work. She cleaned out the stalls, groomed, made up the hay nets, and then went to find Ty so they could start work on Dylan. They took the big bay up to the schooling ring and set out a grid of six poles on the ground to lead him over and around.

As soon as Ty tried to lead Dylan over the poles, the bay stopped and lowered his head to stare at them. Ty clicked his tongue. "Come on now."

Dylan dug his heels in and refused to move.

"Let's do some T-touch on him, right here," Amy suggested.

Ty nodded. They worked over the horse together, making small circles on his face and down his neck until the tension started to leave Dylan's body and his head lowered. As he started to relax, they gradually worked their hands down each of his legs. To finish, Ty picked up each of Dylan's hooves and moved them in slow horizontal circles. As he lowered each hoof to the ground, Amy noticed that he was encouraging Dylan to stand for a few seconds with the toe of the hoof resting on the ground.

"What are you doing that for?" she asked curiously.

"I'm hoping it will help him focus on his feet," Ty said as the horse adjusted his hoof so it was flat on the ground. "He wouldn't usually stand with his toe down, so by getting him to do it, I'm trying to make him think more about where his feet are and what they're doing."

"Makes sense." Amy stroked Dylan's face. His eyes were half closed. "So should we try him over the poles again?"

Ty nodded and led Dylan toward the grid for a second time.

As soon as he saw the poles, Dylan hesitated. Ty spoke to him soothingly, and then, to Amy's delight, Dylan walked on. Nostrils flaring, he picked his way cautiously over the poles. He lifted his feet carefully, but he didn't rush or panic.

"That's a lot better!" Amy said, going around to the other side of the grid and patting Dylan when he crossed the last pole.

Ty smiled and patted Dylan, too. "Good boy."

By the end of the training session, Dylan was walking far more confidently over and around the poles.

"I'm sure this approach will work," Amy said as they led Dylan to the gate.

Ty nodded. "Me, too. But it's going to take time."

"I'd better call Nick and warn him that it isn't going to be a quick fix," Amy replied.

Just then Lou came up to the ring. "How's it going?" she called.

"Fine," Amy replied.

Lou opened the gate for them. "I was thinking," she said

tentatively. "Maybe I could ride Dancer again tonight. But if you're too busy, then that's OK, I can ride another day."

"I've got time," Amy interrupted her. "We can tack up Dancer as soon as we're done feeding."

"Ben and I can do that," Ty offered. "You two go ahead and get Dancer out."

"Do you want to go for a trail ride?" Amy asked Lou. "I could take Storm."

"I don't know," Lou said doubtfully. "Maybe when I'm feeling more confident."

"Come on, let's go now," Amy said. "It's a perfect evening. You'll love riding out on the trails, Lou. Dancer will be good. You know she will."

Lou hesitated and then nodded slowly. It was clear from the look in her eyes that she was excited by the thought.

❧

Once Storm and Dancer had been groomed and tacked up, Amy and Lou rode to Teak's Hill. Initially, Lou looked worried and was tense in the saddle.

"Relax," Amy told her. "Nothing's going to happen. We'll walk as long as you want."

The sun threw dapples onto the sand track through the leafy canopy. Amy could see the tension flow from

Lou. Her sister started to relax in the saddle and enjoy the surroundings.

"It's so peaceful here," she said.

Amy nodded. "I told you you'd like the trails."

"I remember doing this in England when I was younger," Lou said. She half smiled at the memory. "I used to jump fallen tree trunks on Nugget." She patted Dancer's neck and sighed. "I don't think I'll be doing that today." Her eyes met Amy's. "Part of me wants to just canter and gallop like I used to, and yet as soon as I think about doing it, I freeze inside and I can't."

"You'll be able to — it'll just take time."

"I hope so," Lou said quietly.

"You've got to take things slowly," Amy finished.

"But not so slowly that I never improve," Lou whispered to herself, with a slight frown.

Suddenly, the trees opened out and they found themselves riding onto the open hillside. "Oh, wow!" Lou said as they looked out into the valley where Heartland's buildings were nestled next to the mountain. "What a view!"

Amy smiled at her. "Told you it would be more fun than riding in the ring."

"You were right." Lou looked at the grassy hillside that stretched invitingly ahead. "We could try a trot," she said, a look of determination entering her eyes.

"If you're sure," Amy said.

Lou nodded, and they signaled their horses to move forward. Dancer's ears pricked and she broke into a canter. Amy immediately pulled Storm back so that Lou could bring Dancer back to a trot, but to her surprise, Lou didn't. Holding tightly onto Dancer's mane, she leaned forward slightly and let the mare canter on.

"Lou!" Amy called. "Do you want to stop?"

From behind, she could see Lou shake her head, her golden curls bouncing in the wind.

Amy watched as they cantered for about ten more strides, and then Dancer fell back into a trot. Lou bounced in the saddle for a moment, regaining her balance, and slowed Dancer back to a walk.

"You cantered, Lou!" Amy said happily, nudging Storm to catch up with Dancer.

Lou turned to her, and Amy saw that her sister's eyes were glowing. "I did it! I actually did it!" She patted Dancer's neck. "And it felt so good!"

Amy's heart sang. She felt a new connection between them. They had always loved each other, but Lou's fear of riding had been an emotional barrier. But now that riding was something they could share, Amy thought they felt more like sisters than ever.

They stayed out on the trails until the sun was sinking toward the horizon. Storm and Dancer walked calmly on loose reins, their necks warm. Amy found herself chatting to Lou in a way that she would never have done before — talking to Lou as if she were Soraya or Ty. She told her all about Daniel and Amber.

Lou looked at her curiously. "So do you want to be a professional show jumper? I mean, Daddy seems to think Storm's got real potential."

"I'd love it," Amy admitted. "But Heartland will always come first."

"That could be tough," Lou said. "Even Mom didn't do both at the same time."

Amy hadn't thought of that. "I guess she didn't." But then her natural optimism took hold. "Maybe I could."

They rode on in silence.

After a few minutes, Lou spoke again. "Say Storm really starts winning. You're going to want to compete him more and more. How will you find time for that with all the other horses and your schoolwork?"

"I'll manage," Amy said confidently. "I just know I will."

❧

On Saturday, Amy woke up to find that the good weather had broken. It was raining hard, and, after taking one look out the window at the wet ring, she decided that she wouldn't ride Storm that morning after all.

Besides, she wanted to get started on the chores so she wouldn't feel guilty about leaving Ty and Ben when she went to watch Daniel.

Going outside, she thought about the phone conversation she'd had with Daniel the night before. Amber was behaving really well. Amy pictured the roan mare the very first time she'd seen her jumping. She hoped Amber was going to perform like that again.

It was still raining when Ty dropped Amy off at the show. "See you later," he said as she pulled on her jacket. "Wish Daniel luck for me."

"I will." Amy promised. "Thanks for the ride."

"No problem," he said, leaning across the seat and kissing her.

Amy hardly felt the drizzle as she set off across the show ground.

She'd arranged to meet Daniel by the main jumping ring at nine-thirty. He was standing near the gate, watching the class.

"Hi," Amy called. "How's Amber?"

"Much better," Daniel said. "She almost seems back to her old self."

But Amy saw that his eyes looked worried. "That's good news, isn't it?"

"It's not that. It's the ground." Daniel nodded toward the ring. "It's getting really muddy."

Amy frowned. Amber was a heavily built horse. It gave her tremendous power, but it also meant that she'd find it harder to jump in mud. The footing would be slippery.

"The more horses that go into the ring, the worse it's going to get," Daniel said. "There's the rest of this class and then mine — and I'm not jumping until halfway through."

Amy looked at the ring. Already the grass in front of the fences was cut up, the mud showing through in great brown patches. A chestnut was jumping the course. As he turned into the wall, he lost his footing and stopped in front of the fence, his hooves gouging out chunks of the soft turf. She glanced at Daniel and knew that he had seen it, too.

"Daniel!"

They both turned. A stocky man with receding brown hair was coming toward them. He was wearing tan jodhpurs and a navy windbreaker. Amy recognized him. It was Brad Shaffer.

"Brad," Daniel said. "Hi."

Brad came over. "Hey there, Dan," he said, shaking Daniel's hand. "Looking forward to going in?"

Daniel didn't seem to know what to say.

Seeing his difficulty, Amy spoke. "It'll be tough going for a horse like Amber, won't it?"

For the first time, Brad seemed to notice her.

"This is Amy," Daniel said. "My friend."

"Hi," Brad said shortly. He turned away from her and slapped Daniel on the back. "Well, I'd better get going. People to see, you know. Good luck." He winked. "I'll be watching."

Amy frowned. He hadn't even bothered to answer her question about the mud. "Is it really fair to make a horse like Amber jump on ground like that?" she protested as he walked off.

Brad stopped. "Talent is talent," he said. "If Daniel's horse is as good as he says she is, then he won't have a problem. None of the other riders seems concerned."

Amy felt the anger rising inside her at his patronizing tone of voice, but before she could say anything, Daniel spoke.

"But Brad, you've seen Amber. She's heavy — not like the other horses. She's great indoors and even on uneven courses because she's got so much power, but on ground like this, she'll have a hard time finding her footing."

"That's hardly the right attitude, Daniel," Brad cut in, shaking his head. "You're not telling me you can't jump in a little mud, are you?"

Daniel flushed. "Of course not."

"Good," Brad said with a wide smile that didn't reach

his eyes. "Because there's no space in my barn for quitters. You just get in that ring and show me what you can do." He walked off.

Amy swung around to Daniel. "You're not seriously telling me you want to work for him, are you?"

"He's Brad Shaffer," Daniel said.

"So?" Amy said.

Daniel set his jaw. "So if he offers me a place, I'll work for him. He's my way out." He saw her face. "Amy," he said, "I have to get this working pupil position. This could be my one chance to make it to the big time. If I work for him, I'll get to go to shows and meet potential sponsors and owners. And Amber could have a nice stall and the best training. There's no way people would laugh at us if we were part of Brad's team."

Amy wanted to object, but she managed to hold her tongue. She'd already seen enough of Brad Shaffer to dislike him, but Daniel was right. Chances like this didn't come up very often. "I guess," she said reluctantly.

"I'd better get Amber tacked up." Daniel sighed.

Amy watched Daniel warming up Amber. Against the crowd of beautiful Thoroughbreds and warmbloods, Amber, with her mud-splashed roan coat and heavy head, stood out.

"Looks like she should be pulling a cart," a rider on a

dark bay mare called out as he cantered past. Daniel scowled. The boy grinned and cantered on.

Oh, be good, Amber, Amy prayed. *Jump well. Show these losers what you can do.*

Leaving the schooling area, Amy walked over to the main ring. The jumps were just being raised for the Open. Feeling a raindrop on her hand, she looked up. The clouds were gathering. Daniel was tenth in. If it rained any more, the ground was going to be ruined.

Feeling worried, Amy headed back to the practice ring. On the way there she saw the familiar figure of Scott Trewin. Amy stopped in surprise.

"Hi, Scott. What are you doing here?" she asked.

"I'm the show's chief veterinary officer," Scott told her, sounding all official. "I'm standing in for a friend. He was supposed to be doing it today, but his wife had their baby early, so he asked me. And why are you here?" he asked.

Amy was just explaining about Daniel when there was an announcement over the loudspeaker system for Scott.

"Better go. It's going to be busy today with this mud," Scott said as he gathered his equipment and hurried away. "See you later."

Amy continued back to the practice ring and noticed Brad Shaffer with four young riders. They were all smiling at him, and Amy guessed that they were the other candidates for the working pupil place. She stopped at the fence.

Daniel rode over. "So that's my competition," he murmured to her in a low voice.

The loudspeaker announced that the Open Jumping was about to start.

Brad rubbed his hands together. "Well, guys, enjoy yourselves," he said, and turning, he walked into the stands.

The first competitor entered the ring.

A cold wind was blowing. Daniel walked Amber around to keep her muscles warm while Amy went back to the ring to watch the first few entries take on the course. The mud in front of the fences was making it difficult for the horses to take off accurately, and none of them looked as if they were enjoying themselves. Not one of them went clear.

The rider before Daniel rode out with twelve faults. The starting gates opened and Amber cantered into the ring, her head bent against the wind.

"Come on, girl," Amy whispered. "You can do it."

The starting bell went, and Daniel turned Amber into the first fence. The mare didn't hesitate. It seemed as if the *Agnus castus* had worked perfectly. Amber was, once again, the spirited horse that Amy had seen at that first show. Undaunted. Ambitious. Her ears were pricked as she looked at the jump, her whole being focused on it. Quickening her pace, she flew over the first fence.

She came cantering past the stands toward the second jump. Amy could hear the heavy squelch of her hooves as they thudded on the sodden grass. Daniel was sitting lightly on Amber's back, his weight balanced over her withers. Amy could see his lips moving as he whispered words of encouragement to his mare. They flew over the next fence and the next. Soon there was just one fence left to jump — a large oxer.

Amy was on the edge of her seat. *Please let her jump clear*, she thought.

With that, Amber took off and flew cleanly over the spread, landing safely on the other side.

"Yes!" Amy cried, jumping up.

Around her, the crowd burst into loud applause. Patting Amber's neck, Daniel rode out of the ring, a huge smile on his face.

Amy ran to meet him. "That was fantastic!"

Daniel slid off Amber's back and hugged her. "She was fantastic." He gasped, his face wet from the rain. "I could tell she hated the ground, but she just tried so hard. Oh, Amber! You're the best!"

Amber nuzzled his back affectionately.

"You're the only clear round so far," Amy said. "If no one else goes clear, you've won."

"There's still half the class to go," Daniel said. "I'm sure I won't be the only clear."

He was right. Two other horses managed clear rounds, the boy on the dark bay who was also a candidate for Brad's working pupil place and an older woman on a chestnut Thoroughbred.

Amy held Amber while Daniel walked the jump-off course. When he came out of the ring, Amy could see that his face was tense.

"The ground's worse than ever," he said as he mounted. "The mud's really thick. And the turns are tight."

"You don't have to go in," Amy said, looking up as it started to rain again. "You could let the other two jump off and just take third place."

Daniel looked torn. "But I'd lose the position at Brad's for sure. You heard him — there's no place at his barn for quitters. I've got to go."

Amy didn't know what to say. She knew how much he wanted to work for Brad.

"I'd better get Amber warmed up," Daniel said.

Amy headed for the ring. The rain was making the grass slippery. The boy on the dark bay mare was the first competitor in for the jump-off. The mare was a neat, careful jumper, and although she almost lost her footing twice on the turns, she recovered herself and jumped clear.

Amy clapped politely as the boy cantered through the

finish posts, but her heart was in her mouth. Daniel was going to have to really push Amber to jump a fast, clear round if he was going to win.

The loudspeaker crackled. "Our first clear round in the jump-off — that was Carl Carpenter and Go for Gold."

Amy hurried to the collecting ring, the rain hitting her jacket and splashing her face. She wanted to warn Daniel about the places where the mare had slipped. "Daniel!" she called.

Daniel looked around.

Amy climbed over the fence. "The ground's gotten worse at both ends of the ring."

Just then, Carl Carpenter came cantering out of the ring, looking triumphant.

"And now number 165, Daniel Lawson on Burning Amber," the loudspeaker announced. The paddock steward opened the gate and nodded to Daniel.

Amy saw Carl draw his bay up alongside Amber. "You'll never get around on that horse," he said. "Not now that the fences have been raised."

Amy saw a determined look fix on Daniel's face.

"Daniel," she called out.

But Daniel was already riding into the muddy ring.

Chapter Nine

Amy ran to the ringside. *Please let Amber jump a clear round,* she thought as she saw Daniel lean forward and ease the roan mare into a canter. The rain was beating down steadily now.

When the starting bell went, Daniel turned Amber to the first fence. His face was white, but his eyes burned with determination. He was out there to prove just what his horse could do.

Amber sped up into the fence. As her powerful hind-quarters thrust downward, one of her hooves slipped on the mud.

Amy's stomach lurched as the mare flung herself up-ward, every muscle and sinew straining to clear the fence.

She managed it, just barely snapping her hind fetlocks over the top pole. The crowd gave a collective sigh of relief. Amber headed for the second fence, a wide green-and-white oxer. She regained her stride and jumped it without faltering.

Not once did she hesitate as she jumped the next four fences. The trust she had in her rider was complete, and her desire to please him was obvious. The mud sucked at Amber's hooves as the rain lashed down, but she gave it her all.

Just two more jumps, Amy thought as Amber reached the final double. *Just two more jumps and she'll have jumped clear.*

But Amber was tiring. Her breathing was now audible, and her sides were lathered from the effort of jumping in such miserable conditions. As Daniel pulled her into a tight turn before the double, her legs skidded on the slippery grass. Amy knew what Daniel was doing. He was cutting the corner to the fence. It was a tight angle, but it would cut seconds from their time. It was then that Amy saw a pole on the ground, lying several feet in front of the jump. It must have been knocked down in the previous round. Amy gasped. It was right in Amber's way. She would have to break stride to get around it. But then Amy realized that neither Daniel or Amber had seen the pole. They were both focused on the jump ahead, timing their takeoff.

"No!" Amy gasped as Amber suddenly registered the pole and stumbled over it. It was a dreadful moment —

Amy thought Amber was going to fall. But with a desperate push from her hind legs, she seemed to recover. She was just a stride from the fence now — too close to jump it safely. Her hooves sank into the thick mud. She'd have to stop.

But she didn't.

The crowd gasped as Amber flung herself into the air, her ears flattened with the effort.

Time seemed to slow down as Amber hit the top of the fence. She twisted in the air. Then there was chaos as the poles scattered. Daniel fell from his saddle, and Amber crashed heavily to the ground.

For a moment, there was only the sound of the light rain. The mare and her rider lay on the ground, unmoving. Then everything started up again. Stewards raced into the ring. The crowd began to react and rebuild the scene, and Amy, feeling a wave of sickness wash over her, began to run toward the ring entrance.

As she reached it, the gray-bearded paddock steward tried to stop her. "I'm sorry, but you can't go in there."

But Amy wouldn't be stopped. "He's my friend!" she shouted. And rushing past the man, she ran through the rain toward the two bodies.

To her relief, Daniel was moving. Pushing himself up slowly with his hands, he got unsteadily to his feet.

"Daniel!" Amy cried, hope flooding through her. "Daniel! Are you OK?"

He heard her and turned. His face was streaked with mud, and he looked confused. "What — what happened?" he said, looking at the stewards who had just reached him.

But before Amy could answer, Daniel saw Amber lying on the ground. His face began to shudder with horror and concern.

"No!" he shouted as he stumbled toward his horse.

Amy chased after him.

Amber seemed to hear her owner's voice and lifted her head. With an enormous effort she thrust out her forelegs and heaved herself off the ground. But as she did so, her body trembled and she staggered back. When she was still again, she was resting the toe of one foreleg on the ground. It was bleeding badly.

Daniel wrapped his arms around Amber's neck and stroked her softly. "What have I done?"

Amy saw the horror in his eyes as he looked at the mare's injured leg.

"It's going to be OK. I promise," he said desperately. "You'll be fine, just fine. We'll take care of this." Amber nuzzled his shoulder, her dark eyes clouded with pain, but she looked at him trustingly, as if to say, *I believe you. Now you're here, I know I'm safe.*

Amy's gaze met Daniel's, and a look of fear and understanding passed between them. Both of them knew that Amber was badly injured. Not knowing what to say,

Amy touched the mare's neck, her eyes burning with tears.

"Are you all right?" a steward asked Daniel.

Daniel looked at him vaguely. "Me?" he asked, as if that was the last thing on his mind. "Don't worry about me. Where's the vet? We need a vet now!"

"The vet's trailer is on its way," the steward reassured him.

"Maybe you should get checked over," another steward suggested. "We can get your horse into the trailer."

Daniel looked at him as if he were crazy. "I'm not going to leave her. Just get the vet."

The stewards backed slowly away and didn't insist. Soon the white veterinary trailer came trundling across the rain-soaked grass. Scott jumped out and hurried across to Amber.

"Can she walk?" he asked.

"I don't know," Daniel said. He clicked his tongue and pulled gently at the reins. Amber hobbled forward a few paces.

Scott stopped Daniel and knelt down, carefully examining Amber's leg. A grim look came into his eyes. "Let's get her out of this ring — and fast."

✷

A section of the boarding stalls at the show ground had been set aside for veterinary emergencies. Scott drove the trailer there, carefully unloaded Amber, and started examining her properly.

Daniel spoke to Amber constantly, his hands gently stroking her head.

Amy stood silently nearby, ready to help if she was needed but keeping out of the way if she wasn't.

"So what's wrong? How bad is it?" Daniel demanded as Scott finally straightened up.

"It's difficult to say for certain without an X ray." Scott shook his head. "But I think she might have fractured her knee joint."

Amy bit her lip, trying to force back the tears. It wasn't what she had wanted to hear.

"You'll be able to treat it though, won't you?" Daniel said quickly. "So many things are possible now. Legs can mend. She won't have to be put down, will she?" There was a note of desperation in his voice. "There has to be something you can do!"

Amy thought she had never seen Scott look so serious. "We won't know how bad the damage is until we take the X ray," he replied. "If it's her knee joint, then yes, we can probably operate, but you need to know now that she'll never be able to jump at this level again. The joint just wouldn't be able to stand the strain of jumping five-and six-foot fences."

Amy saw Daniel's jaw clench. "I don't care about that," he said. "We don't have to compete. Just as long as she's still with me — that's all that matters. We're a team."

"Well," Scott hesitated, his facing looking grim, "as soon as I've given Amber some pain relief, we'll take some X rays."

ℜ

Amy and Daniel had to wait outside the stall while the X rays were being taken. Daniel's face was set. He didn't seem angry or upset, just numb. It was as if the impact of the accident still hadn't fully sunk in. But Amy understood. He was coping. At the moment, that was all he could do.

At last, Scott called Daniel and Amy into the examining room. Pinning the black-and-white plates up against the light box, he pointed out Amber's injury. It was as he had suspected and Amy had feared — a fractured knee joint.

"A piece of bone has chipped off the joint. The ligament is still attached," Scott explained, pointing out the bones in the pictures. "It is possible to operate. The knee will have to be opened up and the bone screwed back into place. But that's just the start. It'll take many months to heal. She'll have to be confined to a stall for a time, and that's where we can get problems. Some horses simply don't cope with such confinement, but it's vital if the bones are to heal properly."

Amy glanced at Daniel, remembering how he had told her that Amber hated to be in a stall.

"She'll cope," he said grimly.

Scott's face was serious. "Well, the first few days after the operation will be the worst. She'll need to be monitored very carefully, in case infection sets in," Scott continued. "And as she gets older she's highly likely to develop arthritis, which will limit what she can do. At that point, she might need regular doses of anti-inflammatories and painkillers."

Daniel nodded, his lips clenched tight. "I don't care how hard it's going to be. We have to try. I owe it to her."

Scott nodded. "OK. We can go ahead with it, but I just wanted you to know the reality of the situation before we went any further. And we need to talk about the cost, too." Scott hesitated. "It's not going to be cheap. I can be honest with you about that, because I won't be the surgeon."

Amy glanced at Daniel. She'd been wondering how on earth he'd be able to pay for such a major operation.

"I've got a little money," Daniel said to Scott. He glanced at Amy. "I was saving for a new trailer, but that doesn't really matter now. Amber is more important." For a moment, Amy caught a flicker of despair in his eyes, but then Daniel seemed to squash it down.

"OK," Scott said. "The nearest equine veterinary center is about fifteen minutes away. It's not my practice —

I'm just standing in for a friend today," he explained to Daniel. "But I suggest we arrange to have her taken there. The surgical team has a lot of experience in fracture repair, and she'll be in good hands. Now, what about after the operation? Where are you from?"

"Lexington," Daniel replied.

Scott frowned. "That's a long way. I'm afraid Amber won't be able to go home for some time. Should I arrange for her to stay at the veterinary center until she's well enough for the trip?"

Amy saw a worried look cross Daniel's face. She knew what he was thinking. Boarding at a veterinary center would be expensive. She doubted whether he had enough to cover the operation, let alone boarding fees for several weeks. She had an idea. "Maybe Amber could come to Heartland. We're less than half an hour away." Her mind worked quickly. All the stalls were full, but they could turn out one of the ponies. It would only be for a few weeks, and the weather was getting better.

Daniel looked uncertain.

"It would be fine," Amy insisted, just hoping that Grandpa and Lou would agree. She saw the uncertainty in Daniel's eyes. "And you wouldn't have to pay us a thing."

"That would be ideal. It's nice and calm there," Scott said. "I could take over her care and monitor her progress."

"Well, if you're sure . . ." Daniel nodded gratefully to Amy. "Thanks — thanks a lot."

Scott collected the X rays. "OK, let's get Amber ready to travel."

The mare was going to be taken to the hospital in the veterinary trailer — it would be a smoother ride for her than in Daniel's rig. Daniel stayed with Amber while Amy went to get the mare's trailer wraps. On her way back, she suddenly stopped.

Carl Carpenter, the guy who had made the cruel comments about Amber, was leading his bay mare toward the barn. Brad Shaffer was next to him, with his hand on the younger man's shoulder. They were talking and laughing.

Amy felt her blood boil. They didn't look like they'd even given Daniel a second thought.

"It'll be great to have you on board, Carl," she heard Brad say, giving him a firm handshake. "I think we'll make a great team."

Carl grinned.

For one wild moment, Amy wanted to run up to them, to yell at them and tell Brad that what had just happened had been partly his fault. What did they know about being a team? It was Daniel and Amber who knew that, who trusted each other wholly. With the greatest effort, Amy fought the urge to berate Brad and tell him what a small-minded person she thought he was. It wouldn't do any good. Right now she was needed with Amber. She veered past the celebratory pair and hurried back to Daniel.

❧

While Daniel waited for the operation to finish, Amy called Ty from the hospital and told him everything.

"That's such bad news," he said, shocked. "How's Daniel doing?"

Amy glanced to where Daniel was sitting by the coffee machine. His head was sunk in his hands, and he was staring at the floor. "Not good," she whispered. She had a feeling that the reality of what had happened was just starting to sink in. It was going to be a long, slow process for Amber's leg to heal, and there was no guarantee that she would pull through, either.

"Ty," Amy said tentatively, "I've offered to let Amber stay at Heartland to recover. It's only for a few weeks. Do you think that'll be OK?"

"Of course," Ty replied. "But what about Daniel? Where will he stay?"

Amy realized that she hadn't thought of that. "I — I don't know," she said. One thing was sure: Daniel wouldn't go home without Amber. "Maybe he can stay in the guest room. Is Grandpa home? I'd better ask him."

Ty got Grandpa, and Amy explained what had happened. "I was hoping Daniel could stay with us for a while, Grandpa," she said.

"Honey, your friend can stay as long as he wants," Jack said quickly. "It's no problem."

"I guess he'll have to go back to his job sometime soon." Tears stung Amy's eyes. "But I can't imagine him leaving Amber — even for a little while. Oh, Grandpa, it's so unfair."

"Hush, now," Jack said quickly. "Look, tell me where you are, and I'll come over and pick you both up."

Amy gave him directions to the hospital. It was a relief to know that he was coming. She turned off her phone, and, taking a deep breath, she went back to Daniel. "My grandpa's coming over," she said to him. "I told him what happened, and he said you're welcome to stay at Heartland."

For a moment Daniel didn't speak, but then he nodded. "Thank you," he said in a low voice.

"Amber's in good hands," Amy told him.

❧

A few hours later, the news was cautiously optimistic about the operation. "Everything went as planned," Robyn Hartman, the vet who had been in charge of the operation, told them. "Now we just have to wait."

"May I see her?" Daniel asked, his face now clearly showing the strain of the last few hours.

"Yes, but it can only be a quick visit," Robyn replied. "She's back on her feet, but she's still very unsteady after the anesthetic, and we need to keep her as quiet as possible."

"When can we take her to Heartland?" Grandpa asked. He had arrived twenty minutes earlier and was waiting with Daniel and Amy for news.

"Hopefully by tomorrow afternoon," the vet replied. She motioned down the corridor. "If you want to come this way, I'll show you Amber's stall."

They followed her down the corridor and out of the building. Amber was in a padded stall in a large, airy barn. A nurse was in the stall, monitoring her. "Hi, I'm Karen," she said, smiling at them. "Have you come to visit our patient?"

Amy nodded. Amber's head was hanging low, her muzzle almost touching the ground. Her eyes were half closed and her legs looked unsteady.

"Amber," Daniel said softly.

The mare's ears flickered. She raised her head slightly, and, seeing Daniel, her eyes widened and she made an attempt to nicker. He hurried over, his hands stroking and caressing her. "It's all right, girl," he murmured.

Amber sighed and rested her head heavily in his arms.

Daniel swallowed hard. Amy could see that he was biting back the tears as he spoke softly, his face pressed against her head. Grandpa squeezed her shoulder.

"I'm afraid you can't stay long," Robyn Hartman said from the stall doorway. "Karen will call you tonight and tell you how Amber's doing. We'll also give you the number of a direct line so you can call anytime you want. I'll assess her condition tomorrow morning and let you know when you can take her home."

"Thank you," Amy said, realizing that Daniel had hardly heard a word of what the vet had said. She went over to him. "Come on," she said quietly. "We can come back tomorrow. It's time to let her rest now."

Chapter Ten

Daniel said little on the drive back to Heartland. Amy sat beside him, wishing there was something she could say that would help. But she knew there wasn't. Amber wasn't going to jump again. The best that they could hope for was that she would recover enough to be a pleasure horse. All of Daniel's dreams were over.

When they got back to Heartland, Grandpa opened the car door, but Daniel just sat in the pickup, staring at his hands.

"Come on, Daniel," Grandpa said gently. "We're here now."

Daniel looked up blankly and slowly got out.

Grandpa showed Daniel to the guest room while Amy gathered his things from the trunk.

"You look exhausted," Amy said, putting the last of

Daniel's things in the corner of the room. "We'll let you rest. There are some towels on the bed if you want to take a shower. Come downstairs when you feel up to it."

"Thanks," Daniel said quietly.

While Daniel rested, Amy told everyone exactly what had happened at the show. "It was horrible," she said as they all sat around the kitchen table. "It was so slippery, but Daniel had to go in. It was the only chance he had to show Brad Shaffer what he and Amber could do." She shook her head, the image of Amber falling still so vivid in her mind. "I just keep seeing it over and over again. If someone had just put that pole back . . ." Tears choked her voice.

"It sounds awful," Lou said sadly.

"You say Daniel doesn't have any family?" Ben said.

"Not really," Amy said. "It's just him and Amber. That's what makes it all so much worse."

"We'll help him," Grandpa said, putting a comforting arm around her shoulders.

Lou nodded. "You did the right thing bringing him here. Poor guy. I'm glad you were at the show, Amy. He really needed a friend."

Everyone nodded in agreement, and Amy had to swallow a lump in her throat.

Ty stood up. "We should get back," he said to Ben. He

looked at Amy. "You should stay here, we can take care of everything."

"No, I'd like to come out and help," Amy said.

As she followed them to the barn, Ty asked, "What did Scott say about Amber?"

"That she'll have to be confined to a stall for several months if she's going to have any chance of recovery," Amy replied. "She's not going to like that — remember Daniel told us how much she hates being confined."

"Yeah." Ty looked thoughtful. "But if that's the only chance of her leg healing, then we'll have to try it."

Amy nodded, looking serious. "We need to think of ways to help keep her calm so that she doesn't put any stress on that leg. Massaging with lavender or chamomile oil might work, and maybe we could add skullcap and valerian to her feed."

"And comfrey will help the bone heal more quickly," Ty said.

"And basket willow if she seems in pain," Amy added.

Ty nodded and they reached the stable block.

"What is there still to do?" Amy asked.

"We're behind with everything," Ty replied. He began to list the jobs that still needed doing.

Amy groaned inwardly. She'd been hoping to ride Storm, but with so much to do, she'd be lucky to get the chance. Nonetheless, she'd promised Ty and herself that she could deal with going to shows and doing everything else, so now she had to prove it. "That's fine," she said, forcing a cheerful smile on to her face. "I'll go get started."

❧

It was seven-thirty before Amy got to ride Storm. Part of her just wanted to collapse in front of the TV, but she was determined to prove that she could do everything, so she saddled up her horse and rode into the schooling ring.

Storm was as good as ever. As he heeded her lightest signal, moving smoothly through his paces, his neck was flexed, his body round and balanced. Amy rode him into the center of the ring and directed him through a flying lead change, silently thanking the stars that she was blessed with such a perfectly trained horse. She relaxed into the saddle, enjoying the wonderful feeling of the two of them moving as one.

Suddenly, she noticed a figure standing in the shadows near the gate. "Daniel?" she said. She rode over. She was surprised to see him. She had thought he would sleep for hours after the day he'd had.

"Hi," he said with a fleeting smile. "I felt like getting some fresh air."

"How are you feeling?" Amy asked in concern.

Daniel shrugged. "You know." He changed the subject. "That's a great-looking horse."

Storm put his head over the gate and blew softly at Daniel, who rubbed his forehead in greeting.

Amy longed to say something that would let Daniel know she understood. She searched for the right words, but everything she thought of sounded meaningless.

Daniel broke the silence. "I was so dumb," he said, his eyes fixed on the distant trees. "Why did I do it, Amy?" He didn't wait for an answer. "I guess I just wanted to show that Amber had it in her. To prove that she was as good as any of those other horses."

"I understand," Amy said.

Daniel pushed his hands over his face. "It's all my fault that she's suffering."

"It was an accident," Amy said quickly. "If that pole hadn't been there, she never would have fallen."

Daniel didn't say anything.

"You shouldn't blame yourself, Daniel," Amy insisted.

"Yes, I should," Daniel replied sharply. "If I hadn't taken Amber into the ring, then her leg wouldn't be broken now. It's as simple as that." And turning swiftly, Daniel walked back to the house.

❧

By the time Amy went inside after untacking Storm and rubbing him down, there was no sign of Daniel. Jack was in the kitchen, putting the food on the table.

"Where's Daniel?" Amy asked.

"He went upstairs," Grandpa said. "I offered him supper, but he didn't want anything. He said he was going to bed."

"I need to talk to him," Amy said, heading for the stairs.

But Grandpa stopped her. "Let him be alone, honey. He's been through a lot today. You can talk to him in the morning."

Reluctantly, Amy gave in.

❧

The next day, Robyn Hartman from the equine hospital phoned after breakfast and told Daniel that Amber was well enough to be picked up after lunch. When Ben heard the news, he offered to drive Daniel to the show ground to get his trailer and then make the stop at the veterinary center. "It would be no trouble," he said.

Daniel thanked him. "That would be great." He turned to Amy and Ty. "What do you need me to do this morning? I'd like to help out."

"Well, there's still mucking out to do," Amy told him.

"I'll get started on that." Daniel nodded.

Just then, Daniel's cell phone rang. He checked the number. Amy saw him take a deep breath, and then he pressed the receive button. "Hi, Jeff," he said, walking a little way off.

Amy exchanged a look with Ty. They were both wondering how Daniel's boss was going to react to the news about Amber.

Daniel's back was to them. Hunched over, he was talking quickly into the phone in a low voice.

"I guess we should leave him to take care of it," Ty said.

Amy had just started mucking out Jake's stall when she saw Daniel put the phone back in his pocket and walk up the yard.

"What did Jeff say?" she asked, going to the stall door.

"Well, he let me go," Daniel said abruptly.

"What?" Amy stared. "He can't fire you. You haven't done anything wrong."

"In his eyes I have. I told him I couldn't come back for a few weeks — not until Amber's well enough to travel. And he wouldn't let me take the time as unpaid leave."

"Why not?"

"It's the busiest time of the year for him," Daniel explained. "People like to buy horses at the beginning of the summer. Jeff said he needed me back at the barn in the next few days. Either I go or I lose my job." He shook his head. "And I'm not leaving Amber."

"Well, I could look after her," Amy said, trying to think of a way around the problem.

"What's happened to her is my fault," Daniel said. "I'm not going to desert her now. I'll find another job. I don't care what it is, as long as it earns me enough to take care of Amber properly."

Amy tried to be optimistic. "Maybe you could get a working pupil place somewhere else," she said.

"I wrote to all the main show-jumping barns ages ago," Daniel said. "There aren't any spaces available at any of them."

"Well, it doesn't have to be a show-jumping barn," Amy said. "There are plenty of other good trainers around. You could work for one of them and look after Amber. You could probably find another horse after the show season."

"I couldn't afford a horse with the potential to be a top-class show jumper. And I'm not going to just find another horse like Amber. That sort of thing only happens once in a lifetime." Daniel shook his head, his mouth grim. "No, I have to face it. All I wanted, all I hoped for — it's not going to happen. Not now. Not ever. I might even lose my horse." He walked away up the yard.

"Daniel, wait!" Amy exclaimed.

But Daniel didn't stop. He didn't even look back.

Feeling sick, Amy watched him go.

Daniel drove Amber back to Heartland that afternoon.

"Hey, girl, how are you?" Amy said in a soft voice as the mare came slowly out of the trailer.

Amber nuzzled her hands.

Daniel removed the mare's travel wraps, but he left the bandage on her injured leg. Then he led her up to the stall by Storm's. The mare moved stiffly, hobbling on her injured front leg.

Amy tried to hide her shock when she saw Amber's stumbling movements. The mare was in so much pain. Amy turned away, her eyes clouding with tears.

"I hope she settles in soon," Daniel said.

"There are a few things we can do to help," Amy told him. "Dried chamomile or a skullcap and valerian supplement will help keep her calm. You could also try T-touch with her."

"I'd like to. Would you show me what to do?" Daniel said.

"Sure," Amy said. "You just move her skin in small circles with your fingertips. Like this. Gently applying pressure to the muscles underneath."

She went up to Amber and showed Daniel how to make the small clockwise circles, each one in a different place from the last. Daniel watched intently and then tried the technique himself.

"You have to breathe into the circles," Amy told him. "Relax and focus totally on what you're doing."

As Daniel continued to work his fingers over Amber's neck, the mare's head gradually lowered and a long sigh left her.

"That's it," Amy said softly.

Daniel nodded and stepped back. "I'll do some more after I put the trailer away."

Amber put her head up, paced to the stall door, and pressed against it. Then, turning, she hobbled around the stall.

"Hush, girl," Daniel said. "You have to rest."

Amber's ears flickered unhappily. She stepped to the door again, watching him walk away.

❧

By feed time, Amber was no more relaxed. She stared out over her door, her muscles tense, her ears swiveling at the slightest sound.

"Try massaging her with lavender oil," Ty suggested.

Amy brought some from the feed room, and together she and Daniel massaged it into Amber's neck and muzzle.

"She's fine when I'm here," Daniel said. "But as soon as I leave her, she tenses up."

Amy tried to be positive. "She'll calm down soon," she told him.

But something inside her wasn't convinced.

❧

"Scott's worried about Amber," Ty told her when she got home from school the next afternoon. "He doesn't like the way she's always pacing and her leg's swollen up. He thinks the restlessness is the sign of an infection. He's given her some antibiotics, but we've got to keep a careful eye on it."

Amy looked toward Amber's stall. The roan mare wasn't looking out. Ty saw the direction of her glance. "Daniel's with her," he said. "She's calmer if he's there." He shook his head. "She has a long rest period in that stall — at least another two months."

"And if she keeps walking around, her leg's never going to heal," Amy said, feeling concerned.

"Something's not right," Ty said.

Amy sighed and went to Amber's stall. Daniel was massaging the mare with chamomile oil. Amber's eyes were half closed. Seeing Amy, Daniel smiled faintly. "Hi." Very slowly, he took his hands away from Amber. "There, girl," he murmured. "Rest now."

He left the stall and joined Amy. Almost immediately, Amber's eyes snapped open and she tried to follow him, her chest pushing against the door.

"I've been in there for two hours," Daniel said, looking at Amber in distress. "But it's just the same. Whenever I try to leave, she gets really stressed again."

Amy stroked the mare's neck, but Amber ignored her. She wanted Daniel — and only he would do. She reached out and nuzzled at him with her nose.

"I don't know what to do," Daniel said, looking exhausted.

"Come and take a break," Amy said. "Then we'll talk to Ty and see if he can think of anything else to try."

They went to the house. While Amy made them coffee, Daniel sat down with a weary sigh. The local paper was on the table and, finding the help wanted page, he scanned halfheartedly through the ads.

"Checkout clerk, pizza delivery, telemarketer," he read out. "What can I do? I have to get a job soon." His eyes flicked over the page. "Hey, here's one for a barn," he said suddenly. "Stable hand wanted with show-jumping experience, to exercise and groom young horses at top hunter-jumper barn. The zip code is the same as Heartland's. Maybe I should apply for it."

"That sounds interesting," Amy said. "Does it say the name of the barn?"

"Green Briar," Daniel read aloud.

"Green Briar!" Amy shook her head. "Well, that makes a difference. I wouldn't bother if I were you. It's run by the Grants — they're a nightmare. In fact," she said, remembering, "it was Ashley Grant you saw me with at that first show. All Green Briar cares about is how much a horse costs, how much it wins, and what kind of profit it makes on resale."

"Oh," Daniel said, scanning the rest of the paper. "Well, that's the only thing here with horses." He sighed. "Grocery clerk it is, then."

"Something will come along," Amy said softly.

"I hope you're right." Daniel shut the paper. "It's hard even thinking about finding a job. All I want right now is to concentrate on Amber." He picked up his soda and walked outside. Amy followed him.

Amber was weaving, her head and neck moving rhythmically from side to side as she stared out over her door. It was a behavior often seen in horses unhappy at being confined in a stall. When Daniel approached, she stopped for a moment and nickered softly to him. Daniel shook his head. "I hope I've done the right thing," he muttered.

"What do you mean?" Amy asked.

"Getting them to operate on her," he said. "What if she doesn't get better? Then she'll have gone through all this pain for nothing."

"She will get better," Amy said firmly.

"I can't bear seeing her so miserable." Daniel sighed, walking over to Amber's stall. As he walked toward her, Amber stretched out her neck in his direction. Amy had never seen a horse so emotionally attached to its owner.

"It's all right, girl," Daniel said softly. "I'm here now." He placed a hand on Amber's neck, and the mare visibly relaxed again.

Amy went to Sundance's stall. His leg was healing well now, and she had started walking him out in the yard each day so that he got some exercise.

"I just wish there was something more I could do for

Amber," she told him, buckling up his halter. "She's so unhappy."

She led Sundance out of his stall and walked him down the drive. Sundance raised his head to the wind, his ears pricked. "Guess you're glad to be out, aren't you, boy?" Amy said.

Sundance pulled at a patch of long grass at the side of the driveway, and she stopped to let him graze. Looking back toward the stable block, Amy sighed. "I wonder what Mom would have done about Amber," she said to Sundance.

The buckskin pony snorted as he tore at the grass, and Amy felt a wave of sadness as she realized that just twelve months ago, her mom would have been there to answer the question herself, to put her all into helping Amber recover.

She closed her eyes and swallowed hard.

If only I hadn't seen Spartan in that abandoned barn. If only I hadn't begged Mom to go get him that night. . . .

Sundance pulled at the lead rope, and Amy was brought abruptly back to the present, forcing all thoughts of the accident out of her mind.

℮ℯ

Despite the antibiotics, Amber's infection continued to spread. By the next day, her leg was more swollen, and her eyes were lazy and dull. Daniel stayed with her until late in the night. At eleven o'clock, Amy went to find him.

"How is she?" she said, looking over Amber's door.

Daniel was massaging lavender oil into Amber's muzzle. "Not good," he said quietly. "She hasn't eaten anything, and I'm sure the infection's getting worse. Look." He nodded to Amber's leg.

Amber was holding it with just the tip of her hoof touching the ground. The area above and below the operating scar was very swollen.

Amy bit her lip. Daniel was right. It looked bad. "We better call Scott."

"Leave it till the morning," Daniel said. "He's already been out to see her twice today. I don't think there's much more he can do. It's just a case of waiting for the antibiotics to kick in."

Amy looked at his pale face. "Are you coming inside?"

"Not yet." Daniel sighed wearily. "If I leave her she'll only agitate things by walking around."

"I'll stay with her if you want," Amy offered. "You look beat."

"Thanks, but I'll stay here." Amber nuzzled his shoulder. "She needs me. I want to be with her."

Knowing she'd have felt just the same if it had been Sundance, Amy didn't argue. "Well, if you change your mind, come and get me," she said.

"I will." Daniel forced a smile. "Thanks, Amy."

❧

When Amy awoke the next morning, it was just before six o'clock. Remembering Amber in her stall, Amy quickly dressed and rushed outside.

Daniel was still there, sitting in a corner of the stall, his back against the wall. Amber was resting her muzzle on his knees. The skin on her face looked taut and strained.

Hearing Amy, Daniel looked up and narrowed his eyes in order to focus. "What time is it?" he said, sounding disorientated.

"Almost six," Amy whispered, coming into the stall.

"Look." Daniel nodded toward Amber's leg.

The mare seemed more languid than ever, and the scar was now oozing pus. Amy crouched down and gently touched the flesh. The skin was hot and swollen.

"No matter how much iodine I use to clean it out, it doesn't help. The infection is just too deep. And that's not the only thing getting her down," Daniel shook his head. "She hates being inside. You've seen how distressed she is. And she's going to be shut up in a stall for months. How can I put her through this, Amy?"

"Because you love her," Amy said firmly. "Because there's nothing else you can do. Let's get hold of Scott. He'll give her some more painkillers," Amy said desperately. "And maybe he has some antibacterial ointment we can use. She'll feel better then."

❦

When Scott arrived an hour later, Amy could see from the look in his eyes the truth of the situation.

"I can give her another shot of antibiotics and we'll see how she goes, but it's not looking good," he said, softly patting Amber's neck as he came out of her stall. "I'll come back first thing tomorrow and see how she is then, but if she's not any better, we might have to think of alternatives."

"Alternatives?" Daniel's eyes flashed angrily. "What do you mean, alternatives?"

Scott shrugged, looking embarrassed. "You have to think of what's best for the horse." Scott tried to put a hand on Daniel's shoulder, but he shrugged it off.

"I'm not giving up on her," Daniel said. "She'll pull through this. She's stronger than I am. I'm not having her put down."

"We'll see." Scott shrugged, but Amy could hear the hesitation in his words. He was trying to be kind to Daniel, but he clearly didn't want to give him false hope.

❦

Amy woke even earlier the next day. For one small moment, she thought that everything was all right. But then she remembered — Amber. Scott was coming over early to assess her progress this morning. Quickly, she got out of bed, dressed, and ran down the stairs. The first rays of light were slowly sweeping across the yard as she ran into the barn and down to Amber's stall. There, as she expected, she found Daniel in Amber's stall, beside the mare. His clothes were mussed and his face tearstained. At Amy's approach, Daniel looked up.

"How is she?" Amy asked gently.

"She's worse . . . *much* worse." Daniel swallowed. "The swelling in her leg — it feels like fire, and she barely seems to recognize me."

Amy didn't know what to say. Scott's words from yesterday rang in her ears as she reached forward to stroke Amber's neck. The mare didn't move a muscle. Her eyes, always so reflective, were now foggy and listless. It was as though a light had gone out in them.

"I'll go and get her morning grain," Amy said hurriedly. Quickly, she turned and made her way to the feed room. As Amy scooped the food into a bucket, she felt a lump rising in her throat.

When Amy returned with the feed, Daniel was already on his feet.

"Here you are, Amber," he crooned, offering her the mixture.

But Amber didn't even look at him. She just stood there, her eyes half closed.

Daniel blinked, and Amy saw that his eyes were glinting with tears.

"She's not even interested in food," he said. "I've been sitting here thinking, Amy. Thinking about what Scott was saying yesterday. And you know, if you love someone, you don't let them suffer. You do what's best for them."

Amy felt cold. She heard footsteps behind her and was relieved to see Ty's comforting face. She knew what Daniel was about to say, knew what he was thinking, but it was too awful — and a decision that only Daniel could make.

Just at that moment, she heard the slamming of a car door, then feet on gravel. Scott appeared in the doorway.

Slowly, the vet walked forward and gently worked his hands down Amber's legs. Amber didn't move a muscle. As Scott put pressure around the wound, pus spurted through the shaved skin. Scott didn't need to say anything. His face said enough.

"It's bad, Daniel."

But before Scott could go on, Daniel stopped him mid-sentence. "I've come to a decision," he said slowly. "I was stupid to think that a day would make any difference — I know she's in a lot of pain. It would be kinder to — to —"

"We could persevere with fighting the infection," Scott stepped in. "But even if she does get through the infection period, we would still have months of recovery time ahead of us, months of pain, and she might not be any better by the end of it."

"I know."

Standing in the doorway, Amy felt her heart breaking for Daniel. She knew what it was like to have to make such a decision. She'd had to do it herself with Pegasus.

Daniel touched Amber's face. "This isn't fair to you, girl," he whispered. "I can't let you suffer. I can't bear to see you this way." He glanced around at Scott. "Will — will you put her to sleep, please?" On the last word, his voice cracked.

Hot tears pricked the back of Amy's eyes, and she felt a sharp ache in her jaw.

Scott nodded. "If it's any help, I think it's the right decision to make," he said gently. "You've done everything you can to help her, Daniel. No one could have done more. And if this is going to be the way things end — better to do it sooner than to keep her in pain." He touched Daniel's arm in sympathy.

Scott prepared the injection, and Daniel slowly stroked Amber's face, tears coursing down his face. Then as Scott administered the drug, he held Amber's halter and kissed her good-bye.

At first nothing happened, but soon Amber's legs wobbled. She staggered and slowly sank to the floor.

Crouching down beside her, Daniel cradled her head in his arms. "Please forgive me," he whispered in desperation. "Please forgive me," he repeated. "I love you, girl," he stuttered at the last, hoping that she might hear his voice one more time.

The mare's eyelids flickered. For a long moment she stared up at him with a look brimming with love and trust. Then a deep sigh left her and she was still.

Scott put his hand on Daniel's shoulder and spoke softly, "It's OK now, Daniel. She's gone."

Chapter Eleven

It was over. Amy turned her face into Ty's chest. He held her tightly, his arm a comfort as she fought hard to get herself under control. She had to be strong for Daniel's sake. He was the one who needed the support now. Sniffing back the tears, she pulled away from Ty and went over to Daniel, crouched beside Amber.

"Daniel," she whispered, her voice shaking.

He stood up, and without saying a word, he pushed past her and rushed toward the house. To Amy's relief, Grandpa had agreed that she could stay home from school that day. After lunch, she went to try and talk to Daniel, but he wouldn't come out of his room.

"Please," he said through the door. "I just want to be alone."

Amy understood. After her mom had died, all she had wanted to do was shut out the world. So she left him to grieve. Going up to Storm's stall, she put her arms around the gelding's strong, warm neck.

"Why do these things have to happen?" she whispered, resting her cheek against his warm skin.

But she knew only too well that there was never an answer to that.

🐍

That day and night, Daniel stayed in his room. But the following morning, when Amy came back from riding Storm on the trails, she saw him in the yard, pushing a wheelbarrow.

"Daniel," she said, riding Storm over. "How are you doing?"

"Fine." His eyes were bleak. "I've been cleaning out Amber's stall."

Amy stared. "You didn't have to do that."

"Yes, I did," Daniel said, setting his shoulders and continuing up the yard.

Later, Amy spoke to Grandpa about him.

"There's little that we can do at the moment," he said, "except be here for him. I've told Daniel he can stay as long as he wants to." He looked at her in concern. "You look tired."

"I am," Amy admitted. "There's just so much going on — with all the horses and school stuff, and now Daniel."

"And you've been getting up early to ride Storm," Grandpa commented, starting to wash the breakfast dishes.

"I don't mind that," Amy replied.

"Maybe Lou could help," Grandpa said thoughtfully. "She's been saying how much she likes riding again. Couldn't she ride Storm sometimes?"

Amy considered it. "I think he'd be too much for her," she said slowly. "He's really well schooled, but he *is* spirited. If he acted up, Lou might lose her confidence all over again."

"That wouldn't be good," Grandpa said. "Well, maybe in time."

"Yeah, maybe," Amy agreed.

Grandpa frowned. "But that doesn't help solve the fact that there aren't enough hours in the day for you right now."

Amy stifled a yawn. "I'm fine," she reassured him as brightly as she could. "Don't worry about me, Grandpa. I can cope."

❧

Despite her words, however, Amy had to stop herself from falling asleep several times in class that day. She felt exhausted, and it wasn't just because of all the work at Heartland. Every night she was plagued with nightmares about her mom's accident. It would be a year ago tomorrow that it had happened, and, although Amy was trying not to think about it, it was as if a clock in her head was ticking away the hours.

It didn't help when, in creative writing class that day, their teacher asked them to write an in-class essay about the person who had been most important in their lives.

"So who did you write about?" Soraya asked as they packed up their books after the bell. "Was it your —?"

"Grandpa," Amy interrupted her. "I wrote about Grandpa."

"Oh, right." Soraya looked at her quizzically, but to Amy's relief she didn't say anything. Amy picked up her books. She knew Soraya was still worried that she wasn't talking about the anniversary of her mom's death, but she just couldn't. It was far better to try to put it, and the bad dreams, out of her mind.

"Hey, what's the rush?" Ty said as he came across Amy sweeping the aisle of the barn later that afternoon. "Slow down or you'll brush the floor away."

"I'm just trying to get things done," Amy said.

Ty didn't question her any further. With a shrug, he went to the feed room.

Amy put the broom away and was heading back to help him when she saw Daniel coming out of the tack room. It was the first time she'd seen him since that morning. He looked desolate.

"Hi," Amy said. "Ty and I could use a hand with the feeds. Do you have time to help?"

At first Amy thought Daniel was going to make an excuse, but then he nodded and followed her up to the feed room. Ty exchanged looks with Amy. She shrugged. She didn't know why she'd asked Daniel to help, she just felt that it would do him good to start doing things again. As they began to measure out and mix the feeds, she tried to think of something to say, but Daniel broke the silence.

"I've decided to apply for that job in the paper," he said. "At that local hunter barn."

"You mean the opening at Green Briar?" Ty asked.

"But don't you remember what I told you about the Grants? I don't think you'd like them — they're just out to make money," Amy said, astonished.

Daniel shrugged. "That's OK by me. I need to make money. A job where the horses are just business sounds fine to me."

"You don't mean that," Amy said.

"Yes, I do," Daniel said bleakly. "I just want someone to point to a horse and tell me to ride it. Strictly business. That's what I need. I'm applying." He looked at them almost defiantly. He started to mix alfalfa cubes into the feeds.

Amy opened her mouth to protest, but before the words could leave her mouth, Ty had started to speak. "Well, you should do what you think is best," he said to Daniel. "Whatever you decide, we'll back you up."

Amy stared at him. Catching her look, Ty nodded meaningfully in Daniel's direction. Amy's eyes followed his gaze. Daniel was bent over the feed buckets, his face utterly desolate. And suddenly Amy knew that Ty was right. "Green Briar would be lucky to have you," she managed to say, the words cutting through her like knives.

Daniel looked up in surprise. "You mean it?"

They both nodded.

A trace of a smile flickered across Daniel's face. "Thanks," he said, turning back to the feeds. "I appreciate that."

Amy had just come in from the yard for the evening when Nick Halliwell called to check on Dylan's progress.

"He's doing well," Amy told him. "His coordination and balance seem to be improving, and he seems happier. We thought we'd try riding him in the next few days."

"That's good news," Nick said. "I'll stop by this weekend to see him."

"Sure." Then Amy remembered, and she had to choke back the swollen feeling in her chest. "Sorry — Saturday isn't such a good day," she said.

"Fine," he said easily. "Sunday then."

"Good," Amy said with relief. She was about to say good-bye when an idea suddenly struck her. A brilliant idea. Why hadn't she thought of it before? "Nick," she said quickly, "you don't have any working pupil positions coming open, do you?"

"Working pupil positions?" Nick said, sounding surprised. "I don't, I'm afraid. Why?"

"It's for a friend," Amy explained. "You've met him. Daniel Lawson. He won the Six Bar at the Meadowville show. Do you remember?"

"I remember," Nick said. "He was good. But I filled a position just six weeks ago."

"Oh," Amy said.

Nick sounded genuinely sorry. "If anything comes up, I'll let you know."

"Thanks, Nick," Amy said, and she put down the phone. As she turned, she jumped. Daniel was standing in the kitchen doorway. "Daniel!" Amy said, wondering how long he'd been there.

Daniel was frowning. "Who was that on the phone? Why were you talking about me?"

"It was Nick Halliwell," Amy explained. "The show jumper — he owns Dylan. I just thought I'd ask him if he had any working pupil places that you could have. But there isn't anything right now."

"I told you earlier — I'm going to apply for that job at Green Briar," Daniel said abruptly.

"Yeah, I know," Amy said. "It's just — well, there's no need to rush into anything, is there? Grandpa said you can stay here as long as you want. Why don't you wait for a bit? Maybe a working pupil place will open up at another barn."

For a moment she thought Daniel looked torn, but then his jaw tightened. "I don't want to wait. I need the money now." He shook his head. "And I told you, I'm not going to be a show jumper anymore."

Amy stared. "But if there were an opening, I'm sure you'd take it."

"You're sure?" Daniel walked to the table, his face bleak. "Well, I'm glad you are so sure about my life, because I'm not. All I know is that a lot has changed. Everything has changed. I had my chance, and I blew it. It's nobody's fault but mine."

"That's not true. It was an accident, and it did change a lot, but you don't have to give up your dreams," Amy protested.

Daniel looked at her defiantly. "It hurts too much to try to remember my dreams. I called Green Briar after we fed the horses," he continued. "They invited me over for an interview first thing tomorrow." His eyes met hers. "If they offer me a job, I'm going to take it." He turned around and walked out of the room.

Amy watched him go, and as his door shut she sighed wearily and headed back downstairs. Lou was coming out of the living room.

"The flowers for tomorrow arrived earlier," Lou said. "They're on the table if you want to see them."

Amy's stomach lurched. "No, no, it's all right," she stammered.

"Are you sure?" Lou asked.

"Yes," Amy said, and, wanting some air, she hurried past Lou and out the kitchen door.

Chapter Twelve

The rain was beating down, bouncing in the puddles. The sky was dark. A woman was standing by the pickup truck, her blond hair plastered to her head by the rain, her face sad.

"Mom," Amy whispered, moving toward her.

"You asked me to go, Amy," her mom said, shaking her head.

Tears of despair ran down Amy's cheeks, mixing with the rain. "Oh, Mom," she sobbed. "I'm so sorry!"

Amy sat upright in her bed. The gray dawn light was filtering through the curtains. She pushed her hands over her face and took a deep breath. The day had finally come — the day she'd been dreading.

Getting up, she pulled on her clothes and went outside. The morning was cool and fresh, the sun just rising in the sky.

Amy walked slowly up to Sundance's stall. He lifted his head and nickered in surprise when he saw her. She rubbed his golden face and leaned her head against his. He nuzzled her curiously.

I want to forget, Amy thought. *I just want to forget.*

Putting his halter on Sundance, Amy led him outside. His hooves clattered loudly on the concrete, the sound carrying in the silent morning air. Some of the other horses looked out hopefully over their doors as if they thought it might be breakfast time. But as Amy led Sundance over to graze on the grass at the side of the driveway, they lost interest and went back inside their stalls.

A year ago today . . .

As Sundance started to pull at the long grass, Amy sank down on her knees. Shutting her eyes, she began to relive the day exactly a year before. She saw it all again — Spartan abandoned in the barn, the gallop home through the rain, she and her mom heading out in the trailer. . . .

"Amy?"

Amy's eyes sprang open. Daniel was standing in front of her, his face frowning in concern. "Are you OK? I saw you from my bedroom window. What are you doing?"

Amy couldn't answer. Tears choked her. As her eyes

filled up, Daniel's frown quickly deepened. "What's the matter?" he asked.

"Nothing," Amy tried to say, but a sob burst from her. "Everything." She cried incoherently, burying her head in her knees. "Just everything."

She felt Daniel's hand on her shoulder. "Amy — what is it?" he said, crouching beside her.

He sounded so worried, Amy forced herself to explain. "It's my mom. She died. It was a year ago today."

"I — I'm so sorry," Daniel said. He shook his head.

"It's OK," Amy muttered, brushing her tears away with the back of her hand and standing up.

"How did she die?" Daniel asked quietly.

"It was a trailer accident." Amy petted Sundance and forced the words past the painful lump in her throat. "We were rescuing a horse. There was a storm, and a tree fell on the truck." Fresh tears sprang to her eyes. "I talked her into going even though the weather was bad." Her voice choked. "It was all my fault."

"I'm sure it wasn't," Daniel said.

"It was," Amy whispered.

There was a pause. "Sometimes accidents just happen," Daniel said at last. "Deep down we both know that. You just want to be angry with yourself because it's easier to cope if there's someone to blame." He shook his head. "But blaming yourself when it wasn't your fault doesn't help anyone. You helped me realize that."

Amy looked up in surprise. "I-I did?" she stammered.

Daniel nodded. "What you said yesterday. I've been trying to punish myself for what happened." He looked at his hands for a moment. "It was so unfair. Amber deserved so much more. It just seemed easier to cope with her death if I had someone to be angry at — even if it was myself." He glanced at her. "Does that make me sound crazy?"

"No," Amy answered slowly. She knew what he was trying to say. In fact, she was beginning to think that it was exactly what she had been doing over the last year.

"I think that deep down, we want to believe that everything that happens, happens for a reason," Daniel continued. "But it doesn't. Life isn't like that."

Amy nodded sadly as Sundance pushed at her hands with his muzzle. She knew Daniel was right.

"We need to accept what has happened and try to move on."

Amy couldn't speak. Daniel put an arm around her, and she leaned against him.

"Do you think the pain ever goes away?" she asked in a trembling voice.

"No," Daniel replied softly. "But I think it has to get easier. You'll never forget your mom, and I'll never forget Amber. They'll always be there in our hearts, but we have to live our lives. We've got to take what they've given us and move on."

For a moment they were both silent with their memories.

At last, Amy sighed. "Thanks," she said, looking up at Daniel.

"It's OK." Daniel smiled. "Thank you for being there. It's good to have a friend."

"So, are you really going to go to the interview at Green Briar?" Amy asked him.

"Yes," Daniel replied. "It might not be the ideal barn, but right now I just need some time to get myself sorted out, some time to decide what I want to do."

"Does that mean that you might still try to get a working pupil place at a jumping barn one day?" Amy asked hopefully.

"Maybe," Daniel replied.

"So, you haven't given up your dream forever," Amy said quickly.

Daniel shrugged. "Not forever," he said slowly. "But right now, I'm going to take things one step at a time."

Amy smiled. "Me, too," she said.

She patted Sundance. *Yes*, she thought firmly. *Me, too*.

When Ty and Ben arrived, Amy and Daniel were chatting and giving out the morning feeds.

Amy saw Ty's surprised look.

"Daniel looks better," he said when they were alone.

"Yeah," Amy said, nodding. "I think he is."

At nine o'clock, Daniel left to go to Green Briar. He returned an hour later with the news that he had accepted the job.

"Val Grant was eager to take me on when they heard about all my experience in the jumper division," he told Amy when she met him by his pickup. "I think she's planning to develop the jumper side of Green Briar's business. She offered me the job on the spot."

Amy couldn't get too excited by the prospect, but she forced a smile. "Congratulations." She tried to look on the bright side. "At least you'll still be living close by. You can come and visit whenever you want."

"Just try and keep me away," Daniel said. He raised his eyebrows. "And who knows, maybe I'll even be able to convert Val Grant to Heartland's methods one day."

Amy laughed. "Yeah, right!"

Daniel smiled at her. "Look, thanks for everything, Amy. It's been great getting to know you. And judging by the way Storm's been jumping, I guess I'll be seeing you at shows most weekends. It's not going to be long before you and Storm are winning your way around the A circuit."

"Well, I don't know about that. We'll have to wait and see," Amy said. She glanced at her watch. "I should go and get ready. We're going to the cemetery at ten-thirty." She looked at Daniel. "Would you like to come?"

He shook his head. "Thanks for asking," he said. "But I wouldn't feel right going."

Amy understood. After all, Daniel hadn't known her mom. "Sure," she said. "Well, I'd better go get changed."

She went upstairs, but as she pulled a pleated gray skirt out of her closet, she stopped. *Mom wouldn't want us to dress up,* she thought to herself. *She'd want us to go as we are.* Putting the skirt back in her closet, she pulled on her jeans and went down the corridor to Lou's room.

"I'm not dressing up," she said as Lou opened her bedroom door.

"Why?" Lou said, surprised.

"Mom wouldn't have wanted it," Amy answered. "She'd want us to be as she remembered."

"Yes," Lou smiled. "I think you're right."

Twenty minutes later, Amy was standing with her friends and family by her mom's grave.

Grandpa said a few words of welcome and then recited the same poem that Amy had read at the memorial ceremony a year ago. As the words filled the air, a breeze lifted Amy's hair, and she remembered the Native American phrase that Huten, a friend of her mom's, had told her not so long ago: *There is no death, only a change of worlds.*

Mom's gone, Amy realized suddenly. *But her spirit lives on. In me — in everything I do.*

Grandpa stopped talking, and Amy realized he had finished the poem. Everyone began to move away slowly.

Grandpa came over to her. "Are you ready to go now, honey?"

"May I just have a moment by myself?" Amy asked.

Grandpa placed a kiss on her forehead. "Of course." Going over to Lou, he put an arm around her shoulders, and they led the way back to the parking lot.

"Will you be all right?" Ty squeezed her hand.

Amy nodded. She waited until she was alone and all was quiet, then she knelt by the grave. "Mom," she whispered. "It's been a hard year without you. We all miss you very much. But I'm starting to figure things out. I think I understand. I've got to make the most of the talents I have. I'll help any horse that comes my way, whether it's sick or healthy. And I'll ride in shows as well. Who knows — maybe I'll be just like you. Thank you for having given so much of yourself to me, Mom. Thank you."

She shut her eyes. The breeze caressed her hair. It was so gentle, she could almost imagine it was her mom's kiss.

After a moment, she opened her eyes and touched the headstone. *The world's changed now that you're gone, Mom,* she thought, *but I know you're with me in whatever I do, and for all the tomorrows to come, I'll carry on your work. I promise.*

Heartland

Healing horses, healing hearts...

Share Every Moment...